Worry ends where
faith begins.

—An Amish Proverb

SUGARCREEK AMISH MYSTERIES

Blessings in Disguise
Where Hope Dwells
The Buggy before the Horse
A Season of Secrets
O Little Town of Sugarcreek
Off the Beaten Path
Peace Like a River
Simply Vanished
A Stitch in Time
Mason Jar Mayhem
When There's a Will
Shoo, Fly, Shoo!
Earthly Treasures
No Time for Trouble
All Abuzz at the Honey Bee
Home Sweet Sugarcreek
Blessed Are the Cheese Makers

BLESSED ARE THE
Cheese Makers

TRICIA GOYER
&
CARA PUTMAN

Guideposts
New York

Sugarcreek Amish Mysteries is a trademark of Guideposts.

Published by Guideposts Books & Inspirational Media
110 William Street
New York, NY 10038

Guideposts.org

Cover and interior design by Müllerhaus.
Cover illustration by Bill Bruning, represented by Deborah Wolfe, LTD.
Typeset by Aptara, Inc.

Printed and bound in the United States of America
10 9 8 7 6 5 4 3 2

To Lisa Troyer and LeeAnne Heath

Thank you for allowing us to have a glimpse into Heini's Cheese Chalet. What an amazing legacy you are living and sharing with your happy customers!

CHAPTER ONE

R ed and silver ornaments swung from green garland gracing the window of the Swiss Miss. The cold nipped at Cheryl's nose, and she tucked her scarf tightly under her chin. Glancing back inside the shop, she watched Beau turn a slow circle on the Welcome mat.

"I'll be right back. I'm running to Swissters on a quick errand," she explained as if the cat could understand.

Both Lydia and Esther had arrived for what was sure to be a busy morning. Holiday shopping had begun in earnest last week with out-of-town visitors coming for Christmas in the Village, an annual candle-lighting ceremony to honor one of the town's local residents. She'd stood by Levi's side as, at the flip of a switch, the downtown area had come to life with beautiful tree and lighting displays. Even now her stomach warmed as she remembered how they'd sipped hot chocolate and listened to the strolling carolers. *If only I could feel truly at peace at Levi's side without worries of what others think or frets over where this friendship will lead.*

Her black boots squeaked on the snow, and she turned her mind back to what she could be sure of. During the three weeks remaining before Christmas, the Swiss Miss and other Sugarcreek stores would be busier than ever. So would Cheryl as she managed the store, spent time with her friends, and shopped for gifts for her parents and brother.

The *clip-clop* of horse hooves and buggy wheels mixed with the roar of truck engines as Cheryl crossed the street and then hurried down the road to Swissters. It was her favorite cheese shop in Sugarcreek. All of their cheese was made ten minutes away in Millersburg at Heini's Cheese Chalet. In the last year, she'd sent gift baskets from here to family, and it would be the perfect gift for the wedding she would attend tomorrow.

The aroma of coffee filled the air as Cheryl entered Swissters. The coffee bar met her first and drew her in. She paused before it and scanned the festively decorated chalkboard listing the specials, and then she stepped back and shook her head.

"No, let me handle my shopping first, and then I'll get some coffee...," Cheryl mumbled, unwrapping the scarf from around her neck. A brisk Christmas tune played overhead.

She walked to the cheese display to choose some of her favorites of Heini's Cheese and mused that she was both nervous and excited about attending her first Amish wedding. She'd gotten to know Rhoda Hershberger over the last year as Rhoda brought in handmade items for the shop. She made the most beautiful lap quilts and Amish dolls. Before hearing about the wedding, Cheryl had sent Rhoda an especially big order for Rhoda to prepare for the Christmas season, and even with all the wedding planning, Rhoda had managed to fill the order.

Cheryl had many Amish-made gifts perfect for weddings, but Rhoda surely had a hope chest filled with those things. Then

Cheryl had remembered that every new couple had a refrigerator to fill. She picked up an empty handbasket. A few other customers were also filling baskets with cheese and trying the samples. Cheryl knew what most of them already tasted like, but that didn't stop her from enjoying a few samples herself.

She had picked out Colonel Cheddar and garlic-and-herb yogurt cheese when the bell on the front door jingled. She turned, and a smile filled her face as Naomi entered. *Of all the people to run into today.*

Naomi wore a heavy black coat over her Amish dress and apron and a bright red scarf. The pop of color made her cheeks glow—or maybe it was the cold air. Snow flecked the black bonnet that covered her *kapp*.

"Cheryl," Naomi called as she approached. "What a fun surprise to see you here. What are you up to?"

She held up the cheese. "Picking up some gifts. And you?"

"I'm here for a cup of coffee. I've already finished my morning errands. I could use something to keep me warm on the drive back to the farm."

"That's a good idea. I was thinking of getting a cup myself after my shopping."

"Oh, have you tried the olive pimento cheese?" Naomi reached into the chilled case and pulled out a small block. "I bought some the other day, and when I went to get some, Seth had gone through half of it for a snack. I should get more...and then hide it."

Cheryl chuckled, and a lightness filled her chest. "Are you sure it wasn't Levi who got into it?"

Naomi chuckled. "It could have been, the way the two of them eat." Naomi shook her head with a grin. "Sometimes I think they all try to outdo each other."

"A healthy competition I suppose." Cheryl picked up a few more blocks of cheese and added them to the basket. "This should do it for me. If you need to go, I'll let you ring up your purchase first."

"*Ne*, I will walk to the counter with you. I am in no hurry. I only have chores waiting, and I do not mind if they wait longer."

LeeAnne Heath, the store owner, stood still behind the counter. Her head was lowered as if she were deep in thought. Her arms were crossed over her chest, and Cheryl was almost afraid to interrupt her pensiveness.

Cheryl placed her cheese on the counter. "It's sure cold out there."

LeeAnne glanced up and forced a smile. "Is this all today?"

"Well, I was hoping for this to be put into a gift basket and wrapped up..."

"Yes, of course."

LeeAnne rang up the items, and Cheryl paid.

LeeAnne's brows furrowed. "Can I deliver the basket later today, Cheryl? I'm not sure if I'd do a very good job this morning."

"That's not a problem at all. It's for a wedding tomorrow." Cheryl was going to ask LeeAnne if she knew Rhoda then changed her mind. The woman didn't seem to be up for small talk today.

LeeAnne's fingers trembled slightly as she handed Cheryl her change. Tears rimmed the lower edges of her eyelids.

Cheryl tucked the change into her wallet. What was wrong with LeeAnne? Should she pry?

Naomi paid for her block of cheese next. Her concerned glance settled on LeeAnne.

"Is everything all right, LeeAnne?" Cheryl asked.

LeeAnne brushed a strand of brown hair back from her face and let out a heavy sigh. "I'm waiting for a phone call. I've heard some... some horrible news..." The woman's lower lip trembled slightly.

Cheryl waited for the woman to say more, but LeeAnne pressed her lips into a tight line.

Naomi reached out her hand, placing it on LeeAnne's. "How can we help?"

Tears filled LeeAnne's eyes and then spilled over. She quickly wiped them away. "I don't know. I... I'm waiting to hear more. There was a fire this morning. My dad called to tell me."

Naomi gasped. "At your parents' house?"

"No. The cheese factory." LeeAnne's hand covered her mouth. She shook her head in disbelief. "I haven't heard how bad, but Dad said things didn't look good."

Naomi released a heavy sigh and pressed a hand to her heart. "Oh, I am so sorry."

Cheryl shook her head. "Do you need to go to Millersburg? I can cover your store for you."

LeeAnne pointed to the back. "My assistant manager, Janelle, arrived. I heard her come in. I'm waiting for a phone call before I head down. But if you don't mind, I'm going back to check my cell phone—see if I received any more messages."

"We don't mind at all." Naomi pointed to the barista. "We are getting some coffee and will be here for a few minutes. Please let us know how we can help."

"Yes, of course." With a heavy sigh, LeeAnne hurried to the back room.

They walked to the espresso bar and ordered coffee, the happy Christmas music overhead now sounding too cheery.

"Maybe the fire is not as bad as it seems," Naomi offered. "I know all of us depend on Christmas sales to help us through the year... I imagine Heini's is no different."

"I sure hope it's not bad...but..." Cheryl pressed her upper teeth on her lower lips. "If the fire was on the production line, like LeeAnne believes, it can impact more than the holiday season. Who knows how long until they get their cheese production up and running again?"

"True. It's horrible, horrible."

A shuffling sounded behind Cheryl, and she turned. A young man stood there, tall and lanky with a scruffy blond beard. He picked up a jar of mustard off the shelf, but he seemed to be paying more attention to her than the item. He looked familiar in his oversize Army jacket, ripped jeans, and Nike tennis shoes. His bedraggled blond hair stuck out from under a dirty baseball cap. Cheryl guessed she'd seen him around town. But the way he watched her... A chill traveled down Cheryl's spine, and for a moment she wished Levi were here too. One look at Levi's tall frame and broad shoulders and the young man wouldn't think about bothering her.

"What are Seth and Levi up to today?"

Naomi told her about the pruning Seth and Levi were doing around the farm. "Some of our neighbors like to prune their fruit trees in the spring, but my men are not much for sitting still. If there is a task to do, they will not sit around or put it off until later. But I imagine when Levi hears about the fire, he will head down and help."

From behind Cheryl, footsteps neared. It was the young man, and she could hear his heavy breathing behind her. Goose bumps rose on her arms, and she clutched her purse tighter to her side. Surely he wouldn't try to steal her purse or grab her in the middle of a store, would he?

Naomi seemed oblivious to his presence. She smiled as she took her coffee from the barista's hands, but Cheryl couldn't get over the unsettled feeling. It was as if a hundred tiny ants crawled up her arms.

She quickly turned and saw he was still watching them. The young man flashed a nervous smile and then walked away. He moved to the long cooler display with all the cheese and leaned down as if intent on reading the labels.

Cheryl ordered next and paid for her coffee, leaving a generous tip. She was about to tell Naomi she'd walk her to her buggy when LeeAnne approached the counter again with the assistant manager by her side.

"So it's bad?" Janelle was asking.

"Worse than I thought. Dad said that I wouldn't recognize the production area. His phone was getting bad reception, and he's supposed to call me back from a landline, but from what I heard there's nothing that can be salvaged."

"Nothing?" A horrified look flashed across Janelle's face. "But what about…?"

The ringing of the store phone interrupted LeeAnne's words. Without hesitation she picked it up. "Yeah, Dad. It's me." Then as she listened, the color drained from her face.

CHAPTER TWO

Cheryl moved toward LeeAnne with Naomi by her side. Janelle gripped the woman's arm as if worried LeeAnne would faint. Then, through pursed lips, the words none of them expected emerged.

"They think it's arson?" LeeAnne gripped the phone with one hand and the counter with the other. "And what about the cultures? Please don't tell me they're all gone too."

There was silence as she listened, then she grimaced. "Dad, wait. Am I hearing you correctly? All our cheese cultures have been d-destroyed?" LeeAnne's lower lip quivered as she held the phone to her ear. "Yes, I'll be right there." She hung up the phone and then lifted her face. Her eyes focused toward the ceiling tiles, and her brow creased as the news sank in.

Cheryl took a step toward the counter. "Would you like me to drive you there? I don't think it's safe to be driving when you just heard news like that."

"No." LeeAnne shook her head. "My husband... He's on his way." She turned to Janelle. "Can you watch the store for the rest of the day? Lock up tonight?"

"Yes, of course." Janelle wrapped her arms around LeeAnne, but LeeAnne stood tall and stiff, still processing what this meant for her family, for her store, for their cheese-making business.

Then, with a quick hug in return, LeeAnne rushed to the back room and gathered her things. Not a minute later, she was climbing into the front seat of her husband's truck, her face emotionless.

Janelle put on her apron and looked to Naomi. "I've worked in retail for most of my life, and I understand how to sell cheese, but I don't know the production aspect. It sounds like losing the cultures is a bad thing."

Naomi nodded. "*Ja*, very bad. The cultures are what give the cheese their unique characteristics. The cultures from Heini's were brought over by LeeAnne and Lisa's ancestors from Switzerland at least a half century ago. The cheese cultures are like a sourdough bread starter. A little bit of the culture starts each batch of cheese. Without the cultures, they have lost everything. It affects the whole family. It impacts Lisa and her dad's business down at Heini's, and LeeAnne's here..."

"But more than that, the whole community," Cheryl added. "That cheese is as much a part of our community as any other product."

Janelle shook her head. "But arson? Who would have done that?"

Cheryl wondered the same. Who would want to ruin the manufacturing of such wonderful cheese? A competitor? That was her first guess.

A clatter sounded from the next aisle, and Cheryl jumped. She looked over and saw the young man watching her again. With jerky movements he swooped down to pick up the cheese grater he'd dropped, placing it back on the shelf.

She eyed him boldly this time, hoping he'd get the hint he didn't intimidate her. His eyes darted to Janelle behind the counter, back to Cheryl, and then he hurried to the front door. The bell on the door jingled as he opened it, and he gave one last awkward glance back before rushing out.

Outside the door, the man removed his hat and brushed his bangs out of his face, and then he hurried to the parking lot and climbed into an old, dinged-up gray truck.

Something stirred inside Cheryl. Curiosity. Suspicion. *Something is up. He's involved in this somehow.*

Cheryl nudged Naomi's arm. "Did you see that guy who left?"

Naomi twisted one of her kapp strings around her finger. "Ja, he acted strangely, did he not?"

"Maybe he knows something. Maybe...he's involved," Cheryl whispered the words into Naomi's ear, and the woman's eyes widened.

"You think so?"

"I'm not sure, but something tells me I need to capture his license plate. We need to know who he is..."

She pulled her cell phone out of her purse and rushed toward the front window. She typed in her phone's password and then quickly took a few shots as he drove away, hoping the photos weren't too blurry. He sped down the road, rushing to make it through a yellow light. Did he see her taking his photo?

I hope he did. I hope he knows someone's on to him.

Overhead the song "Silent Night" played, but instead of giving Cheryl peace like it usually did, she cringed. Things would be more silent for Lisa, LeeAnne, and their family this year. What could they do to get things up and running again? When could they go back to cheese making... or could they? Would this be the end to their cheese making all together?

Cheryl turned to find Naomi standing behind her with a puzzled expression on her face. She was holding her paper cup of coffee and Cheryl's. One eyebrow was lifted. "I think you have watched too many cop shows on that television of yours," Naomi stated plainly.

Behind Naomi, Janelle was also eyeing her, her head tilted to the side, as if trying to figure out what was happening.

Cheryl released the breath she'd held. "Don't give me those looks. Didn't you think he was acting strange?"

"A little," Naomi admitted.

Janelle shrugged. "He was probably curious, that's all. It's not every day you hear about a local business burning to the ground."

Cheryl reached out and took her coffee from Naomi and took a sip. "That's true, but don't you think I should at least tell Chief Twitchell about my suspicions?"

"Do you have time for that?" Naomi fiddled with the top button of her coat with her free hand, trying to fasten it. "It is the Christmas season, and I know things are busy around the shop."

As if on cue, a few more customers entered, and Janelle called out a greeting. "Welcome to Swissters, let me know if I can help you."

Cheryl waved a good-bye to Janelle and walked toward the front door. Naomi walked by her side. Cheryl didn't want to argue with her friend, but something deep down told her not to let it go so easily. But Naomi was right, now wasn't the time. She needed to get back and check on Esther and Lydia over at her store.

"I suppose things are picking up at the Swiss Miss. More than the normal rush of Christmas customers, there should be a few deliveries today. Still..."

Obviously guessing what she would say next, Naomi swept her hand, motioning to the store. "Surely whoever the arsonist is, he or she would not be here after starting the fire. It would not be smart of him."

"That's true." Cheryl nibbled on her lower lip as they stepped out into the cold day. "And if he is involved, he wasn't too smart drawing so much attention to himself." She offered Naomi a quick hug and then watched as the woman gingerly held her coffee to the side as she climbed into her buggy. Naomi rested the coffee cup on the floorboard as she tucked the lap blanket around her and picked up the reins.

"See you at the wedding tomorrow," Naomi called. Then she picked up the paper cup with one hand and held the horse's reins with the other. "I am glad you will finally attend an Amish wedding. I suppose you are eager to see one."

Cheryl nodded. "See you then." She watched as Naomi waited for a big truck to pass and then motioned for her horse to pull out. She offered a final wave, unsure if her friend saw her.

Then with quickened steps she crossed the street. She paused slightly to watch Naomi's buggy as it crested the hill out of town. As pretty as the scene was, she couldn't imagine driving one. She was so spoiled being able to climb into her car, turn on her heater with a push of her button, and then listen to her favorite Christmas tunes drifting out of the car's speakers. Not to mention the ability to drive a lot faster than a horse and buggy.

Her boots crunched on the dirty, crusty snow as she walked back toward her store. A smile touched her lips. No matter how many cases Naomi had helped solve over the last few months, it was still the woman's nature to believe the best in people—even ones acting suspiciously.

Could the young man have been involved?

Cheryl hurried down the busy sidewalk then paused, wondering if any of her photos turned out. If they didn't, then there would be no worries over whether she should show them to the police chief.

She pulled her phone from her pocket and checked the photos. Three were blurry, but the last one looked pretty good. She pulled off her glove with her teeth and then used her fingers to zoom in on the photo. The image of the back of the truck grew, and she adjusted its position to get a better view of the license plate. Yes, it was clear. She could read all the letters and numbers. It was an Ohio plate—an older version—but she could make it out.

Even though Naomi thought Cheryl was jumping to conclusions, she decided to show the chief later today. If Cheryl had learned anything in her time in Sugarcreek, it was that while things weren't always how they appeared, sometimes they were. And sometimes the most obvious clues to solving a crime were right under one's nose.

CHAPTER THREE

Cheryl had just tucked her phone back into her pocket when it rang. Was it Lydia or Esther telling her to hurry back to the shop to help? She glanced at the number and saw that it was her mother.

It was early in Seattle still, and her mother usually called later in the day. Cheryl's heartbeat quickened as she answered.

"Hello, Momma. Are you okay? Is everything all right?"

"Cheryl, I'm fine, but you sound...cold. Do I hear your teeth clattering?"

The cold wind nipped at Cheryl's nose, and she resumed her walk. "It's, uh, a little cold here. I ran out for a wedding gift."

"That's what your car is for, dear. Remember how you used to get so many ear infections when you were little? Remember to wear a hat, even when you're going out for a minute or two. Your ears are sensitive."

"Is that why you're calling, Momma, to remind me to wear a hat?" She chuckled.

"Not at all. Oh!" Her mother's voice rose an octave. "I want you to check your e-mail. I signed you up for a special Web site. It was a little pricey, but I think the service will be worth it."

Cheryl's brow furrowed. She paused her steps. "The service?"

"It's a Christian dating site called e-Love. My friend's daughter joined a few years ago, and she was engaged to a wonderful man within nine months. Now she's married and expecting twins!"

Cheryl resumed her steps. "A dating Web site? Momma, you signed me up for a dating Web site? Don't you know that's where all the creepy guys hang out?"

"Oh, please. I looked into it first. They have a good filtering system, and my friend's son-in-law is not creepy. He's a very nice young man."

"But a dating Web site? Momma, really. How desperate do you think I am?"

"I didn't say you were desperate. I realize you appreciate your life in Sugarcreek very much. I also know that you have a special friendship with that handsome Amish man. But you know, Cheryl, your biological clock is ticking. It's not as if you have many more years to figure this out. And if that young man is interested in you, he's taking longer than a buggy driving cross-country to tell you so."

Cheryl reached the front of her store but paused before going inside. The last thing she wanted was for Esther and Lydia to overhear this conversation. It was bad enough that her mother used the "your biological clock is ticking" comment, but even worse that she pulled Levi into it.

"Mother...I honestly don't know what to say to all this. Please tell me that you didn't spend a lot of money."

"It was a pretty penny, but I'm doing it for you. I want to know you're happy and taken care of. And is it too much for me to wish for grandchildren someday? Hopefully Matt and Nicki will bless us with some, and hopefully you will too." Her mother's words were followed by a long sigh—one that Cheryl knew well.

Another cold winter wind slipped down her neck, and Cheryl bunched her scarf under her chin. "Tell you what. I'll look into it when I get home tonight...but I'm not making any promises."

"Of course not. It's not like I'm expecting an engagement by New Year's or anything. Take a look around. Read a few profiles. See if there is anyone—tall, dark, and handsome—who catches your eye."

"Fine, but I need to go now. The shop looks busy."

Cheryl walked into the Swiss Miss, and the aroma of cinnamon from one of the burning candles greeted her.

"Get back to your work. But please call me tonight and let me know if you find anything interesting."

"Yes, Momma. Love you." She quickly hung up. The store did look busy. Two ladies were chatting as they sniffed candles, and a man was holding an Amish doll, eyeing the stitching. Cheryl overheard Lydia helping him.

"All our dolls are made in our community. We do not order them from someplace else, and they are not factory reproduced. In fact..." Lydia grinned. "The young woman who made this doll is getting married tomorrow, and I believe these will be the last bunch of dolls we will have from her for the rest of the year. She and her new husband will be visiting family in Pinecraft, Florida, leaving next week."

Lydia's words must have convinced him because the man picked up not one but two dolls and hurried to the counter. Esther helped another woman by the quilts, and Cheryl quickly removed her coat. She fluffed up her hair from where her hood had pressed it down and hurried over to the woman at the cheese display in a refrigerated cooler. The cheese was made by the Millers and a few other families. She'd thought about wrapping up some of their cheeses for a gift, but it seemed tacky to give things from her own store, as if she were too cheap to buy something elsewhere.

"Can I help you?" Cheryl paused by the woman's side.

The woman glanced up, and her face was red, troubled. There was something in her gaze—anger or worry—that made Cheryl guess that she was going through a hard time.

"Yes, please do." The woman's words were rushed. "Do you have any of Heini's cheese? Many stores carry it."

"No, but we have Katie's Buttercream Fudge, which is made down at Heini's. I also have some other wonderful cheeses. One of my favorites is a soft cheese made by..."

"No, thank you." The woman's words cut off Cheryl's. "I'm only looking for Heini's cheese. I'm buying all I can." She hurried to the door.

"You might want to look..."

The woman stalked out before Cheryl had time to finish.

"You might want to look down the street," Cheryl finished even though the woman was long gone.

Lydia finished helping her customer and then approached Cheryl's side. "Well, that was interesting."

"Yes, and she missed out. I was going to tell her that Swissters is just down the street, and they have display cases filled with the cheese, but she didn't give me a chance."

"Or she can drive down to Heini's." Esther chuckled. "It is only ten minutes down the road."

"Oh!" Cheryl's eyes widened, and she reached forward and grabbed Esther's arm, gripping it gently. "You two haven't heard, have you? There was a fire at Heini's and..." Cheryl paused, noticing not only Esther and Lydia listening, waiting, but the women by the candle display too. Because of that, she decided not to share all she knew. Her guess was word of the fire would soon be out, but the news was often slow in reporting suspicions of arson until the police gave them permission.

"There was a fire at Heini's, and it doesn't look good," Cheryl stated briefly. Shock flashed on both girls' faces, and the customers pelted Cheryl with questions. Was the fire big or small? When did they expect it to reopen? There was much they didn't know yet.

Lydia crossed her arms over her chest and pulled them in, clearly troubled. "It would be a shame for such a wonderful business to lose all the Christmas sales. How did you even find out?"

"There isn't much to tell," Cheryl responded. "I was shopping at Swissters when LeeAnne got the call. I'm sure there will be more about it on the local news tonight..."

Esther and Lydia looked at each other, dismayed. They didn't have televisions and couldn't watch the local news.

"I can fill you in on what I hear at work tomorrow," Cheryl said, trying to appease them.

The customers finished their shopping and checked out. Soon the shop was quiet again.

"I still can't believe there was a fire," Esther said as she straightened the shelf of Amish dolls. "I wonder how it happened." Before Cheryl had time to tell the young Amish girl any more of what she'd heard, Lydia's voice rang out.

"Speaking of fire, you should look over here! The carpet— Cheryl it is a mess. It is covered with soot and ashes."

Cheryl hurried over. Sure enough, black footprints tracked from the floor to the cooler case and back again. She bent down and picked up a piece of the soot. It was thin and fine, and the odor of smoke filled her nostrils.

Lydia approached with the sweeper and began to sweep it up. "That woman's boots must have been covered with a lot of soot to leave this mess. And it must have been fresh too, otherwise it would have been knocked off by all the snow on the ground."

"It's almost as if she'd walked through a really sooty area and then got in her car and drove straight here," Cheryl commented.

"Yes, but where would she have picked up so much soot?" Esther wondered out loud, but even as she said those words a realization hit Cheryl.

The three women looked at each other, and Cheryl released a sigh. "Do you think there is any chance that woman was at Heini's Cheese Chalet?"

"She would have had to have been close to the fire to pick up all of that." Esther's voice was low.

"The only problem is," Cheryl said, moving to the front window to glance out and scan the sidewalks, "we have no idea who that woman was or where she came from."

Cheryl looked up and down the sidewalk. There was no sign of the woman. Cheryl turned back to the others. "Or why she wants to buy up as much Heini's cheese as she can."

Chapter Four

The afternoon remained steady yet calm as customers came in and out of the Swiss Miss. Many were looking, but the cash register kept up a steady tempo. Cheryl spent most of her time going from customer to customer helping them find the right treasures from the many the Swiss Miss had to offer.

She was in the middle of helping two women from out of state who were looking for one-of-a-kind gifts when Lydia caught her attention.

"I am sorry to interrupt." The girl flashed a smile at the customers. "There is a call for you, Cheryl."

"Thanks. I'll leave you ladies in Lydia's capable hands. She'll help you find the perfect gifts." The ladies nodded then started asking Lydia questions.

Cheryl walked toward the office, keeping an eye on the pulse of the store as she passed through. The couple by the candles looked like they'd settled on an armload of the fragrant gifts. Esther was ringing up several lap quilts for a man who had a big grin on his face. Apparently his Christmas shopping was done early.

When she entered the office, Cheryl found the phone on her desk. "Hello. This is Cheryl."

"Cheryl, I need your help." The woman's voice was slightly frantic and quite rushed. "I've completely let the day get away from me, and if I don't get a gift over to the police station before five o'clock, I will never hear the end of it."

"How can I help?" Cheryl bit her lower lip and hoped the woman's name would come to her quickly, but that might require the woman to actually slow down and take a breath.

"It's Delores's birthday. She mentioned it earlier this week and sounded lonely. I thought it would be nice to surprise her with a gift basket." Janie Henderson. That's who this was. Sounded like something that successful businesswoman would do. "I meant to get something for her myself, but a horse got colic and my time evaporated. The important thing is that she gets the basket and that it's anonymous. I don't want to embarrass her or anything."

"It sounds like a wonderful idea." Cheryl might have to pitch in something of her own. "What were you thinking about?"

"Oh, the typical. Books. Gift cards. Coffee. That's why calling you was the better idea. I'd like it to be something fresh and different. It'd be way too boring to be a blessing if I was left to do it."

Cheryl was glad she didn't have to hide the grin those words brought out. "How much do you want to spend?"

Janie stated a number, and Cheryl began cataloging what she could put together that would hit that range. One thing she loved about the Swiss Miss was the wide variety of products. Truly something for everyone. "I can have something ready in an hour."

"Is there any way you could deliver it? This horse is doing better, but I still can't leave her."

"I'd be glad to." It would be the perfect excuse to mention the man from Swissters, as well as the odd woman with the ash-covered shoes, though she knew a lot less about her. Cheryl took the payment information as well as what to write in the card—with a note to keep it anonymous—and then got to work on the basket. She couldn't help but wonder what happened between Delores and Brandon Richardson when they went out on the date Delores had seemed so excited about just last month. Things must not have worked out between them if Delores was feeling lonely. It was sweet that Janie had sensed Delores's loneliness and wanted to make sure she had a basket of goodies for her birthday. It was always nice to be remembered on special days.

Cheryl wrapped the basket in a layer of cellophane and then tied it with a large lilac ribbon. The wire running along the edges kept the bow's shape as she picked it up.

"That is a beautiful basket, Cheryl."

"Thank you, Esther." She felt pleased. Now her prayer was that the basket would bring joy to Delores on her special day. The fact it gave Cheryl an opportunity to share her concerns about the fire was secondary.

Since Lydia and Esther were handling all the customers with ease, Cheryl slipped on her coat and then wrapped a scarf around her neck before pulling on gloves. She grabbed the basket and headed to the door with it.

"I'll be back in a few minutes. I need to deliver this for a client. Shouldn't take too long."

Esther waved. "We will be fine."

They would. Those young women were a godsend when it came to operating the Swiss Miss. They cared about the specialty shop almost as much as Cheryl did and knew the products better than she did even after running the shop for nearly a year and a half.

Cheryl stepped outside. The bite of winter air had her taking an unexpected deep breath that practically froze her lungs. She shifted the basket to one arm and then tugged the scarf higher until it covered her nose too. Kathy Kimble, the owner of the Honey Bee Café, waved as she hurried into her shop. The combination of cold and time were enough to keep her moving as rapidly as the slick sidewalks allowed.

Cheryl kept her eyes on the sidewalk, only looking up to cross the street. There were a couple of breakable jars of jelly in the basket that wouldn't survive a slip and fall. Fortunately it was only a couple blocks down Main Street from the Swiss Miss to the police department. When she reached the front door, Cheryl again juggled the basket to free one hand to open the frosted door.

Delores Delgado, the police station's receptionist, sat behind her old metal desk. Her eyes widened and jaw dropped as she looked at Cheryl. "What's all this?"

Cheryl smiled as she approached the woman. "A birdie told me it was your birthday and asked me to deliver a basket filled with gifts. Happy birthday, Delores."

The woman slipped her black glasses up her nose and then glanced around. "*Shh.* I don't want the word getting out."

"Really? Birthdays are an event to celebrate." Cheryl pasted on her brightest smile as she said the words.

"Maybe when you're your age." Delores harrumphed, but a telltale gleam lit her eyes. "Is that really for me?"

"Yes, ma'am. That's what the card says." Cheryl pulled it from its nest of cellophane and handed it to Delores with a flourish. "I'm pretty sure that's your name."

Delores nodded, her dark frizzy hair bobbing out of control. "I didn't think anyone would remember."

"I'm glad that someone did and that I got to create and deliver the gift." She shifted the basket onto the desk. Delores reached for it then put her hands in her lap as if unready to believe it was really for her.

"Is, uh, Chief Twitchell in?"

"Sure. You barely caught him though. He has to leave for some meeting or another."

"Thanks. I'll head back there."

Delores shook her head as if rousing herself from a stupor and picked up her desk phone. "You will not. It may be my birthday, but I'll make sure he's available before you go waltzing back there."

"Yes, ma'am." Cheryl mumbled the words as Delores dialed in a number.

Delores relayed the request into the phone and nodded. "He says you can go back."

"Happy birthday again."

Delores waved her off, but her gaze never left the basket and the treasures nestled inside. As Cheryl walked past the desk into the larger office area, she could hear the woman talking about the items. Sounded like she'd nailed what to include in the basket.

She pulled off her gloves and loosened her scarf then ran her fingers through her short hair before approaching Chief Twitchell's small office. She rapped on the door frame, and he looked up before waving her in.

"Hello, Cheryl. Staying busy at the Swiss Miss?"

"You know the Christmas season. It keeps us moving." She sank on to one of the green vinyl chairs in front of his desk. "Did you go to the fire out at Heini's today?"

He studied her carefully. "So that's what this is about? Can't say I'm overly surprised. One of these days I should make you an officer."

"Oh no!" Cheryl held up her hands in front of her. "I'm content running the Swiss Miss. But I was at Swissters earlier today when LeeAnne got the news of the fire. She said there was thought it was arson?"

"The fire is outside my jurisdiction, Cheryl. It's over the line and in the Millersburg territory, but I've talked to the Millersburg chief and the fire investigator. Too early to say for sure, but the fire investigator seems to be leanin' that direction."

"A slow day around here?"

He guffawed. "Hardly. But a lot of families here are impacted even if just until Heini's can reopen."

"Do you think reopening is possible?"

"We'll know for sure once the fire zone cools and experts can get there and see how much damage was done. The good news is that most of the equipment is stainless steel, so it should be salvageable."

Cheryl nodded. "That is good news. When Naomi and I were at Swissters, a young man seemed very intent on listening to everything we had to say about the fire." She paused, wondering just when he would tell her to leave the investigation to the professionals. Well, she'd started, she might as well see where her thoughts would lead. "I know it's a stretch, but I wondered if he could be involved somehow. I took a photo of his truck's license plate as he left. Took off in a huge hurry too." She pulled out her phone and brought the photo up before turning the phone so the chief could see the image.

He sighed as he glanced at it. "Cheryl, you know I can't investigate every person you think might be involved in a possible crime. We don't even know if there was one yet."

"I understand. But his actions were very suspicious."

"I'll jot the plate down."

"Thank you." She waited as he pulled out a pocket-size notebook, and she started to recite the number.

Chief Twitchell froze and then looked up at her. "Repeat that number again."

Cheryl did so, curious why it mattered.

"That's the license number of a truck that belongs to a young man who is suspected of being involved with arson at a local farm about twenty minutes from here." Chief Twitchell turned to his computer and typed in some information before turning the monitor toward her. "Does this man look like the one you saw?"

A driver's license photo was on his screen, all the other information blocked out. Cheryl leaned closer to study it. While clearly a couple years younger in the photo, it certainly looked like the young man who kept hanging on their conversation at Swissters. "It sure looks like him."

"Interestin'." Chief Twitchell leaned back in his chair and picked up his notebook. He made a notation before turning his attention back to Cheryl. "Was that all you had for me? Though this is a lot. We've been looking for that young man for a month. It's good to know he's still in the area."

"Can you tell me who he is?"

"No."

Cheryl hadn't really expected him to tell her, but she wished he could. Before plunging on, Cheryl took a deep breath. "There was also a woman at the Swiss Miss who was desperate to buy Heini's cheese, but I had none. She took off muttering about buying all the cheese she could. What was really odd, though, was the pile of ashy footprints she left behind."

"Did you get her name?"

"No, but I'll keep my eyes open for her. Maybe she stopped at some of the other shops in town."

"Maybe. Or maybe she just really likes Heini's cheese. She wouldn't be the only person." Chief Twitchell didn't seem too interested in her, though Cheryl was grateful he'd taken her seriously on the young man.

"I agree, but the soot. It was left by someone who had walked through a lot of it recently. Recently enough the snow outside didn't remove it." She shrugged. "It made me think the Heini's fire would be the only one that fit the description that I've heard of recently."

"I understand, Cheryl, but without a name, there's not much I can do." He launched to his feet and gestured to the door. "I appreciate you comin' in. Some of this information was very helpful. You can rest assured we'll take it from here."

"Thank you, Chief." Cheryl wrapped her scarf around her face and headed back outdoors. Would the chief follow up on the crazy cheese woman?

Or should I?

CHAPTER FIVE

It was almost closing time when Cheryl returned to the Swiss Miss. She was relieved to know she'd been right about the young man, but the police had better things to do than track down a woman who had sooty shoes. If she thought that was a clue, Cheryl would have to track it down herself.

The bell jangled as she entered the shop, and her Amish assistants looked at her with tired grins on their faces.

Lydia tucked a loose strand of hair behind her ear then adjusted her kapp strings. "It is about time for us to head home."

"We have straightened most of the store." Esther straightened a tablecloth that had ridden up under the matching Amish dolls. "But we can stay if you need us."

Cheryl could hear the longing in their voices. The girls were great employees, and days like today would work anyone off their feet. She glanced around the store, and while it wasn't pristine, the gals had done an admirable job keeping up with it. The store didn't have any customers, and there were only a few more minutes before she'd turn the shop's sign to Closed.

"Go ahead. I'll come in early tomorrow to attend to the few things you haven't already taken care of. Thanks for your help today."

"You are welcome." Esther's smile bloomed. "There is a Singing at one of the homes tonight. It will feel great to put my feet up for a few minutes at home before we leave."

Lydia needled her with an elbow. "And you think our *maams* will not have us working from the moment we walk in the door? You are daft. See you tomorrow, Cheryl."

The girls whirled through the front door in a swirl of dark capes and bonnets. Before the door could shut behind them, LeeAnne's sister Lisa Troyer yanked it open. Her steps were measured as she entered the Swiss Miss and her ready smile absent. She carried a small basket wrapped plainly with a simple bow.

"Is that my gift basket?" It must be. It looked perfect for a Plain wedding.

"It is." A small smile tipped Lisa's lips. She was tall with dark hair and blonde highlights, bright blue eyes, and a small cleft in her strong chin. Her usually bubbly friend couldn't find her smile. Cheryl could understand.

"I'm so sorry about Heini's."

Lisa set the package on the broad counter and then sagged against it. "I think I'm still in shock, but not as much as LeeAnne. That's why I'm here delivering the package rather than her. Her husband had to take her home."

"It must be a terrible loss. I hear there's a story about how your family came to the area."

"Yes, Heini's has been in our family for generations. But we've been cheese makers since the late 1880s. My grandfather John Dauwalder and great-uncle Krist began making cheese then. When they immigrated to Holmes County, they apprenticed." She sighed again. "It's so hard to believe that their legacy is gone." She paused then shook her head. "We don't know that it's completely gone yet. It just looks very bad."

"Surely it's not. You and your sister are still here. There must be insurance, and you can rebuild." Anything else was a terrible thought.

"I wish we could, but our cheese cultures were destroyed in the fire."

"Can't you get more?"

"There are cultures out there, but not our cultures. Each cheese culture is unique. They each have a distinctive flavor that's developed with care and time. If we lose one, then we adapt and create a new one. But to lose all of them?" She sighed again and leaned even harder into the wood counter. "Heini's could buy cultures from somewhere else. We can clean the equipment that wasn't destroyed in the fire, we can rebuild what was destroyed, but we've lost our heritage, our cheese."

"That's terrible!" Losing the cultures sounded so much worse than damage to a building and equipment that could be replaced and fixed.

"I kept hoping we'd get a call saying we were mistaken and the investigators found the cultures. But Cheryl, there's no way they could have survived that fire."

"Surely if they were in a refrigerator they were protected."

"Cultures are so delicate. They have to be maintained at precise temperatures and fed at the perfect intervals." Lisa rubbed her eyes. "When my great-uncle Krist bought Heini's from the original owners in 1925, I don't think he had the vision for all that it and Sugarcreek would become. It was my father who started offering cheese samples in our store. When he took ownership from Krist, Dad innovated in a way that brought people." She shrugged. "Who doesn't like to sample before they buy? Yes, Dad was the one who did that."

"And you still do it today."

"Yes, I've seen that sell more cheese than the prettiest displays and the best staff."

"One bite and people are sold."

Lisa's face crumbled. "There won't be anything left to sample now."

"If there's anything I can do..." Helplessness knotted around Cheryl's heart as she said the words. She meant them, but she didn't have unique cheese cultures in the office that she could give to her friend.

"I appreciate it. Right now your prayers matter most."

"You know you have those."

"Thank you." Lisa straightened. "Well, standing here complaining won't change a thing. Time to get back to work." A small smile traced her lips, making Cheryl think of the Amish proverb that Naomi had said more than once, "Pray not to have easier lives; pray to have stronger backs."

"Thank you for your listening ear. You know, my dad is a kind man, but he is not without enemies. I wonder if one of them was behind the fire." Lisa shifted away from the counter. "See you around."

Cheryl opened her mouth to ask exactly what Lisa had meant about her father having enemies, but a couple of middle-aged women walked in as Lisa headed to the door. She didn't want to ask in front of people who didn't know Lisa and her family. "Thank you for the delivery."

Lisa waved, but then wiped her cheek as she continued to the door. Cheryl's heart ached for her friend. It was a terrible load to carry. The possible death of a business in this instance was also the death of a dream and a family legacy. The thought tightened her chest.

Marion Berryhill slipped in behind the two women. She quickly approached Cheryl, her dark, short hair tucked underneath a cap. "Cheryl, I need your help. Eden turned one last week, and you wouldn't believe the number of flashy, loud toys she received. I told my siblings they'd better watch out because I will be delighted to return the favor at their kids' next birthday or Christmas."

"I can imagine it's noisy at your house."

"You would not believe it. And the number of batteries those toys consume is scandalous. Someone ought to call a government agency and report those companies." Marion paused as if gathering her thoughts. "Anyway, I was thinking one of your Amish lap quilts and dolls would be perfect."

Cheryl glanced at the shelf of the plain, pale dolls. "Uh, Marion, I don't think I have one with your rich skin tones."

Marion laughed as she pushed up her coat sleeve revealing flawless ebony skin. "I know you don't, but we do live in Sugarcreek and this will be part of Eden's heritage."

Cheryl couldn't help grinning at her friend, whose perspective was always so refreshing. "Then come right this way. I have only a few lap quilts left. They've been selling like crazy, but there's one in beautiful pinks and mint that would be perfect for Eden."

In a moment, Marion was rubbing the quilt's fabric as she *ooh*ed and *aah*ed over the beautiful color combinations. It was perfect for her Eden. Cheryl agreed and looked over for Lisa, but her friend had disappeared. She'd have to track her down later to ask more about Lisa's father's enemies.

As she rang up Marion's items and then helped the other ladies find the perfect candles and lotions for secret sister gifts, Cheryl couldn't completely forget the tragedy that had befallen Heini's.

After she locked the door and flipped the sign to Closed, she looked around the store but decided waiting until the morning to clean made better sense. Right now she was too disturbed by what Lisa had told her about Heini's cultures to be concerned that a doll was out of place here and a doily out of place there. All of that could be righted in no time in the morning. Unfortunately, Heini's problems didn't have a simple solution.

No, that would require a lot of good old-fashioned police work and some luck to solve.

As her beautiful Siamese cat came out from his hiding place in the office and wound around her feet, Cheryl wished she could do something meaningful to help her friends. Prayer mattered. She knew that. But sometimes it would be nice to do something more.

She grabbed a pad of paper from the top of the counter next to the cash register. "Just a minute, Beau, and we'll bundle up and head to the cottage."

First she jotted a note to herself. She wanted to make sure she asked Lisa about her father's enemies but also wanted to ask if Lisa had heard of people going store to store to buy up Heini's cheese. Maybe this wasn't the first time the woman had done it. Or maybe she was doing it because of the fire.

CHAPTER SIX

The cottage held a chill that settled in Cheryl's bones as she set Beau's cat carrier on the hallway floor. She shoved the front door shut behind her and headed straight to the thermostat. The crazy thing was set at sixty-two. No wonder the rooms tipped toward frigid. She adjusted the temperature and then let Beau out. He quickly wound between her legs and then led the way to his food bowl. He sat pointedly in front of it, deigning to spare her a glance. She chuckled as she bent down to rub his silky head.

"Fine. I'll get you fed before I figure out what I'm going to eat." After she filled his bowl and refreshed his water, she turned toward the cupboards. Those shelves might be lined with food, but the thought of cooking for one, yet again, depressed her. Her thoughts strayed to Levi as she opened the cupboard doors. What was he eating tonight?

She pulled out a package of spaghetti and jar of sauce. It would be so much nicer to prepare this for both of them. But the fact they'd admitted they cared about each other in a way that could easily be more than friendship did not mean that they had the freedom to do anything about it. Instead, they'd agreed to let things continue as they were.

As she filled a pan with water and added a dash of salt and splash of olive oil, she wished they hadn't been so practical.

Men hadn't lined up at her door since her engagement had ended, but she hadn't exactly encouraged them either. Maybe her mom was right. Maybe she did need to do something more than wait for the right person to miraculously appear on her doorstep. It didn't help that she'd met Levi almost the first moment she'd arrived in Sugarcreek.

He wasn't perfect; no man was.

But he was dependable and thoughtful, had a deep love for God, and was always willing to help anyone who needed him. Those were wonderful characteristics in a man. Add his personality and looks to the mix, and it was no wonder her thoughts strayed to him. No wonder she compared others to him.

The water began to roil, so she added the noodles and focused on preparing her small, humble meal. After she'd eaten and cleaned up, she decided she could sit and stew about how unfair life could be or she could do something practical.

Sitting around and simmering in emotions wasn't really her style, so she pulled out her laptop and a notebook to jot down her thoughts. Lisa Troyer had given her some background on cheese making and how delicate cheese cultures were, but she didn't fully grasp it. Nothing a little research on the Internet couldn't help her figure out.

It didn't take more than a couple of minutes to learn that cheese cultures helped ripen the milk. You could buy cheese cultures on the Web, and each type of culture produced a different type of cheese. Want Italian cheese? Then you should try a thermophilic culture. Then came the next question, should you use a DVI or a mother culture?

Cheryl's eyes glazed a bit as she read until she realized Heini's must use mother culture to maintain consistency across batches. That would require a stable environment, one that a fire would destroy. It also meant that if the mother culture was destroyed, the exact same cheese could not be reproduced.

As Cheryl read, her stomach rumbled. *Could I make cheese?* The Web sites made it sound so easy, but she shook her head. Buying Heini's wonderful cheese was even easier. All the attention to cleanliness and only using stainless-steel pots, double boilers, and more pretty much ensured this was outside of her league and expertise.

She had dug into a new Web site when someone pounded on her front door. She startled and then set her laptop next to her on the couch. "Coming. Just a minute."

Her phone told her it was almost eight. Who could be at her door? She didn't normally get a lot of company at home, especially the uninvited kind. She peered through the window next to the door, and her stomach danced and flipped. She quickly brushed her fingers through her hair then unlocked the door with a grin.

"Seth and Levi? I didn't expect to see you tonight."

Levi grinned at her, and her heart sped up. "I hope it is a good surprise."

"Of course. Please come in."

Seth glanced from his son to Cheryl and back again. "We have brought something for you. Something this young man is convinced you will like and need."

Cheryl looked to Levi for an explanation. "Oh?"

He crossed his muscular arms across his shirt and studied his father. "Do you mind holding the door for us?"

"Of course." Cheryl opened the door wide and stepped out of the way. What was Levi up to? The excitement in his eyes made it clear he was eager to show her something.

Levi and Seth stepped away from the door, and a moment later she heard huffing. Then they hefted a Douglas fir and carried it through the doorway. Seth had the pointed top while Levi grunted under the trunk.

"Levi, it's beautiful! And perfect." Cheryl clapped her hands as the fragrant aroma of the fresh fir began to fill the living room. "And huge."

Levi shifted the tree trunk with a grunt. "You should have seen the ones we left behind. Where would you like it?"

"I'm not sure. I don't think I even have a tree stand."

Seth snorted. "That is why we have one on the porch."

Cheryl hurried to the porch and found a bag from the local hardware store. Inside was a fresh tree stand as well as a couple of boxes of electric lights. She smiled at the completeness of the thoughtful gesture. After pulling the tree stand from the box, she looked around the living room. Right in front of the window would be the perfect place for the beautiful tree. She pointed. "Let's put it there."

Levi slowly lowered the trunk to the floor, then Seth set the top against the wall. "I see one problem with that location, Cheryl." Levi took off his hat and ran his hand through his hair before replacing the hat. "That big ole couch is in the way."

"Small problem." She waved a hand at the couch. "I've moved it on my own. I'm sure you two can slide it to the side without sweating."

Seth shook his head, and a small smile escaped on his usually solemn face. "Only you, Cheryl." He turned to Levi. "Let us move it before she creates more ideas, Son."

It only took the men a minute to shift the couch and create a space perfect for the tree. A pine aroma filled the air. Wide branches splayed out like green-patterned lace, tiered in layers. Cheryl stared at it filling the window, and her throat tightened. Only a really good friend would think that she needed a Christmas tree. And only an exceptional friend would find such a perfect tree and bring it to her and then move her furniture. Was she wrong to wish they could be more and to hold hope for that possibility?

Levi glanced from her to the tree. "Do you not like it?"

"I love it." As she turned to smile at him, tears clouded her sight. "It's perfect. Thank you."

A slow smile grew on his face, and he thrust a hand over his heart and playfully collapsed against the wall. "You had me worried. That somehow I had made a mistake."

"This is no mistake, Levi." She turned to Seth. "Thank you for your help getting the tree and bringing it here. I can't wait to get in Aunt Mitzi's attic and find the perfect ornaments to decorate it."

"It was no trouble."

Levi turned back to the tree. "If you like it, we should lock it into the stand."

"Wonderful. Thank you."

He dropped to the floor and crawled under the tree.

Cheryl turned to the older man with the long beard that fell to his second button. "Do you know anyone who works at Heini's?"

Seth nodded. "The community is small. Even though they are not Amish, the owners have been a key part of Sugarcreek for nearly one hundred years." He made a clucking sound. "Terrible what happened there today."

"I haven't been able to get it out of my mind all day. I was actually doing research when you arrived to see if the cultures could have made it, despite the fire."

Seth sank on to the couch. "I do not believe there is any way the cultures survived. I worked there as a young man. True, things have likely changed, but I do not think even technology could have protected them. The cultures were coddled, even back then. We were told repeatedly that if we ever touched them to handle them with extreme care. If anything happened to those original cultures, then the cheese people expect from Heini's would cease to be."

"What was the cheese making like?" Cheryl sat across from him and focused on Seth's animated face.

"It is such a delicate process. That is what surprised me most. Even then the cultures were held in a secure, refrigerated environment—one that a temporary worker like me did not get to enter." He leaned forward and placed his hands on his knees. "Since I never was even allowed close, all the precautions seemed unnecessary."

Levi pushed out from under the tree. Clumps of fir needles clung to his hair, and Cheryl resisted the urge to brush them away.

Feeling her chest tighten at Levi's nearness, Cheryl turned her attention back to Seth. It was safer that way. "So, uh, only the cheese makers had access?"

"Ja. That is the way it was managed then. Heini's treated the cheese-making process with utmost care. Each culture is a living thing. If you properly care for it and feed it, it will propagate as long as you need."

Cheryl wrinkled her nose. "I don't know if I like the idea of propagating cheese."

Levi burst out laughing. "You are definitely a city girl."

"That's true. I'll never look at cheese the same way."

The men laughed with her, but then she sobered as the reality of the cultures being destroyed hit her afresh.

"So now that the cultures have been destroyed, what will happen to Heini's?"

Seth shrugged. "The cultures will have to be replaced or there will be no more cheese. Even then it will never taste the same. Heini's will never be able to recreate what was lost."

CHAPTER SEVEN

Cheryl's car looked like a bright blueberry in a sea of black pebbles as she parked her car in the open field in Millersburg. Amish buggies parked around her in every direction. She looked around, wondering if she could pick out Levi's buggy. It was impossible. Even though many varied in size and style, there were just too many.

As she exited the car, her feet crunched on the snow and her foggy breath hung on the air. She glanced at the gift basket on the front passenger seat and decided to leave it there for now. She didn't know how gifts were handled—or how English guests were handled for that matter. To add to that, she'd never attended such an early morning wedding, or one on a Thursday. Today would be full of all types of new experiences, and as much as she wished to have someone by her side, to experience the rhythms of life, it was not to be. Cheryl simply straightened her shoulders and headed toward the large house and barn, deciding to enjoy the day without a mind full of what-ifs and why-nots.

Up ahead on the crest of a small hill, a group of Amish men stood in a cluster. Cheryl walked by where they were standing and stopped short. The first thing she saw was the trail of vehicles parked down the road. They were mostly vans, driven by the

English drivers who gave rides to those not in the immediate area. Should she have parked there instead of with the buggies? Cheryl guessed that she probably should have, but it was too cold to head back and move her car. Hopefully they'd understand that she didn't know better. But beyond the rows of vehicles she saw something else that caused her heart to ache. Cheryl sucked in a cold breath, and the chill moved down her neck and moved through her arms.

Just down the road, a blackened building rose up from the white landscape, like an ink blot on a white canvas. Cheryl's lower lip trembled, and her hand covered her mouth. It was Heini's. She had no idea that the wedding would be so close. The sign was still clear to read, untouched. Part of the building was still standing, but some of it had crumbled and was nothing more than a charred mess of broken beams. A few vehicles were parked around it, and barriers had been set up to keep people back.

Naomi had told her before that family and friends of the bridal party gathered for two days prior to a wedding to prepare all the food. After all, most Amish weddings had between two hundred and six hundred guests. How sad it must have been for them to be preparing for such celebration knowing their neighbors and friends down the road were facing such loss. Cheryl hurried past the men and said a quick prayer for LeeAnne and Lisa and their families. No matter how the fire started, its devastation was the same. She also prayed for Rhoda and her soon-to-be husband, Ezekiel Byler.

Lord, make this day special for them. May those in this community see the beauty of a new marriage despite the ashes, and may they be able to find joy in the midst of the mourning.

Cheryl crossed her arms over her jacket and pulled them toward her as she walked. She hurried toward the group of people gathering outside the shop door. Since Amish met in homes for church services instead of church buildings, it was no surprise that the wedding was held at a home too. And in the biggest part of the home, which was the shop. She'd heard of some Amish weddings being held in barns, and she tried to imagine the crunch of fresh straw under her feet as she walked toward the person she loved.

She shook her head and pushed those thoughts out of her mind. She didn't want to think of that now. Think of him—Levi.

Instead, she joined the line of people entering the shop. She didn't recognize any of those in line and guessed they'd come from out of the area. Even though it was cold outside, as soon as she passed through the doors the warmth from the body heat of many guests met her.

Immediately, she noticed the usual seating arrangement for Amish gatherings. Everyone sat on long wooden benches without backs. Men sat on one side of the building. Younger boys sat with their fathers, and older men sat in the back. On the other side were the women and girls. And despite the number of people, it was strangely quiet. She scanned the men's side looking for Levi. He'd most likely be sitting by Seth and maybe his brothers—although the younger men were sitting near the front. Nearly everyone looked the same in the dark jackets, white shirts, and dark hats.

There were no arches with tulle or candelabras with white candles and flickering flames. There were no large flower bouquets—just a small table with a vase of flowers at the front.

Cheryl looked around, hoping to see a familiar face. *Where should I go?* Then she spotted it—the women's section. While most of the people in attendance wore Amish clothes, a small cluster of about twenty people in non-Amish clothes were seated in the back right corner of the shop. Cheryl hurried that direction.

An older lady that Cheryl recognized from church pointed to a seat next to her. Cheryl removed her heavy coat and then sat. As she glanced around, she noticed a mix of sadness and concern on their faces, not typical expressions one saw at a wedding.

The older woman brushed a strand of gray hair from her forehead and leaned close, whispering to Cheryl. "Did you happen to see the fire damage?"

"Yes. It's horrible, just horrible." The woman's friend commented before Cheryl had a chance to answer.

Cheryl sighed. "I feel so bad." She kept her voice low. "They not only lost their manufacturing area but their retail business too." She squirmed in her seat. "I'm not sure what I'd do over at the Swiss Miss if we faced such a thing."

Cheryl looked around. They were the only ones whispering. A few of the Amish women in the row in front of them cast disapproving glares over their shoulders. Cheryl straightened in her seat and decided not to talk. She didn't want to get kicked out of her first Amish wedding.

"I've heard a rumor that it might be arson." A voice behind Cheryl spoke near her ear. She turned. An older man in glasses sat there. Didn't he realize that he was sitting on the wrong side of the room and that no one else was talking? His thick lenses made the man's eyes appear twice as large. Next to him sat Sandy Schlesman from Sugarcreek Sisters Quilt Shoppe, and Cheryl guessed the man was Sandy's husband.

Sandy scooted forward on the wooden bench to get closer to Cheryl. "I was worried they were going to change locations for the wedding," Sandy whispered.

"Why?" Cheryl mouthed. "Because they were afraid it would put a damper on the wedding?"

"Oh no, more than that." Sandy's brow furrowed, speaking low. "Because Ezekiel's father, Alvin Byler, is one of the cheese makers at Heini's. Can you imagine seeing the place you've worked all your life in flames the day before your son's wedding? Yesterday when he watched it burn, he no doubt ached for his friends and coworkers, but he probably mourned his loss of a job too."

"That must have been so hard." Cheryl's mouth circled into an O. "Was there any place they could have moved the wedding instead?"

"He's the only one with a shop big enough. The property was passed down by his father, who was a furniture maker," another guest chimed in. "They had to have it here. It's too bad that he no longer has a job though."

The older Amish woman in front of Cheryl cleared her throat. Cheryl turned back around and straightened in her seat, getting the hint.

A moment later, an older Amish man stood up at the front of the gathering and blew a long note from a pitch pipe. Almost as one, those seated on both sides stood. In unison, young and old together, their voices rose in song. They sang in German, and each word was stretched into long syllables. Everyone knew the words, but those in her section just watched.

The song lasted ten minutes. When the last note trailed off, Cheryl watched and waited. Would they sit or sing another song?

The song leader hummed a nasally hum. Cheryl covered her mouth, attempting to keep herself from snickering. Everything was new and different. Even though some of her best friends in Sugarcreek were Amish, there was so much about their customs and traditions that she didn't understand. Standing in the back, with her red dress and high black boots, she felt more out-of-place than she had in a very long time.

After the songs, Rhoda and Ezekiel entered through the side door, followed by a group of attendants. The bride didn't look much different than when Cheryl saw her in the shop. She wore her white kapp and a new blue dress. The other young men and women also wore blue.

Next was a long sermon, and Cheryl couldn't understand a word of it. As the minister spoke, everyone was quiet and attentive. Well, except for the older men in the back who'd fallen asleep.

After the man had been speaking almost an hour, the Amish woman seated in front of Cheryl pulled out a packet of cookies and offered them to her two daughters. Cheryl's stomach rumbled, and she wished she'd brought a snack for herself too. *Wouldn't that get some disapproving looks.*

Her gaze must have been intent on the cookies because the youngest girl lifted her hand and stretched a cookie Cheryl's direction.

"Oh no," Cheryl whispered, waving her hand. "Ne." She offered the girl a smile instead.

"Cheryl." Sandy tapped her from behind and then pointed to the front. "They're doing the marriage ceremony now. You're almost missing it!"

She paid closer attention and watched as the minister talked to the couple. She didn't understand his words, but the tone in the building changed. Smiles filled the guests' faces. A few of the women wiped tears of joy from their eyes.

Cheryl considered other weddings she'd attended. The music, the vows, and the kiss at the end were always so romantic. She thought of her own dreams of marriage as a young woman. She'd always imagined standing before witnesses one day and sharing her vows—committing herself to another person for a lifetime. *Will I ever have that for myself?*

As she watched, the couple got on their knees before the minister and bowed their heads. She leaned forward to pay attention, and her purse at her feet buzzed. Embarrassed, she quickly reached into her purse and grabbed her phone. Someone had sent her a text. Again the Amish woman in front of her turned around and frowned.

The couple up front was now standing, and Cheryl glanced down at her text, making sure it wasn't an emergency. LOOK AT

THE DATING SITE, AND IT'LL BE THE BEST CHRISTMAS GIFT YOU CAN GIVE ME. LOVE, MOMMA.

Cheryl shook her head and sighed. She deleted the text and turned off the notification. Then she slipped the phone back inside her purse. *Great timing, Momma.*

She lifted her chin and focused again on the wedding ceremony. They were still speaking in German, and even though she couldn't understand the words, the love between Rhoda and Ezekiel said it all.

Surely God has good plans for me too. She had to trust that. She had to trust Him. But today wasn't the day to focus on what she was missing. Instead, she simply needed to focus on celebrating this couple and the new life they were starting…and staying awake during a ceremony where she could hardly understand a word.

Chapter Eight

The ceremony ended, and Cheryl sighed. It was beautiful without all the elaborate decorations and fuss. Why spend tens of thousands of dollars on a dress and decorations? It made no sense after seeing the joy in a simple wedding like this. It was so clear that Rhoda and Ezekiel adored each other with a pureness that made Cheryl want to weep happy tears. She prayed that love would carry them through the many ups and downs, highs and lows that would come in a life lived together. The burned-out shell of Heini's across that road proved that this life was full of lows. What was the Scripture that said a man was promised trouble? At the same time God promised to never leave nor forsake His children. She prayed that promise would carry the couple through every moment that was to come.

She followed the stream of older women and mothers with younger girls who moved to one side of the shop. As she watched, a group of men grabbed tables from outside and set them up with chairs. A mobile kitchen was also parked outside the side door, and a stream of women carried in dishes of food, arranging them on the table. So full were the tables that Cheryl hoped they wouldn't buckle under the weight. There were casserole dishes with stuffing and potatoes, bowls of fried chicken, peas, coleslaw, baskets of rolls, a variety of salads, and two long tables filled with pies—oh, so many pies!

As the reception food and tables were being set up, Cheryl stopped and chatted with many people. She knew more people than she realized and discovered she was being woven into the fabric of this community in a way she hadn't expected when she moved to Sugarcreek.

Even though she'd sat separately during the wedding, there was no separation now. These people accepted her and welcomed her, and she loved them for it.

Cheryl said hello to Daniel and Ruthanna Yutzy and then said a quick greeting to Anna Byler who promised she was bringing in another delivery of her marvelous soap that week. Cheryl thanked her since the Swiss Miss's supply was reaching destitute levels. She'd turned to locate someone calling her name when she was tackled around the waist with a bear hug from cherubic Gracie Yoder.

"Well, hello to you too, Gracie."

Gracie grinned up at her before running off to hug Bishop Ebersol.

"You are the popular one." A familiar deep voice caught Cheryl's attention.

She turned to face him, and her heart pounded in a quickened beat. Without a hat, his blond hair fell across his forehead. The hair at his temples was damp with sweat from moving tables, yet his eyes sparkled upon seeing her.

"Levi! I wondered if you'd be here today."

"Of course. Our families have been friends for generations. I had no thought of not attending." He stepped closer to her, and Cheryl let herself get caught in his cobalt gaze. "Would you like to sit with us? Maam sent me over to see." Cheryl loved the way he called Naomi his maam even though his biological mother had died when he was a child.

"I would love to. Thank you. And thank you again for the Christmas tree. My living room smelled so good this morning." They walked side by side through the crowd until they reached a table surrounded with Millers. The tables had simple white tablecloths and jars of celery as centerpieces in the middle. Cheryl greeted Naomi with a quick hug before settling down on the bench at the far end. Her seat was precarious enough. One puff would send her sprawling on the floor. Still, she was secure in the presence of this family that had embraced her as one of their friends.

Eli and Caleb were teasing Elizabeth and Esther, taking turns tugging on their kapp strings. The Miller family delighted in the nonwork-time togetherness. This family knew how to work hard but also how to rest well.

Naomi's gaze caught Cheryl's, and she smiled as she nodded to Levi. A slow heat climbed Cheryl's neck. She never quite knew how to interpret gestures like that. Did it mean Naomi thought they should be more than friends? Or was it her way of letting Cheryl know she was aware of their growing closeness?

As much as Cheryl wanted to interpret the gesture as Naomi's approval of their close friendship, she was certain anything more would be doomed. She was English, and he was Amish. As witnessed today at the wedding, the church made it clear that the two shouldn't mingle—not in church services, not in weddings, and definitely not in marriage. The desire of the Amish to be apart and separate from the world was a boundary Cheryl dared not attempt to cross. No matter how her emotions urged her to do so.

Cheryl sighed, and Levi turned slightly toward her. "Everything all right?"

"Weddings always make me sentimental." She smiled at him as she shrugged. "There's something about two people pledging their forevers to each other that makes me..." She searched for the right word. "I don't know. But it makes me happy and a little sad too."

A calm knowing filled his eyes, and he nudged her shoulder. "That is all right. Most events have a happy side colored with a bit of sadness. It is the nature of life and makes the happiness even greater."

Or tinged it with melancholy. Cheryl shook the thought away and gazed around the room. "So what should I expect from this part of the festivities?"

"Oh, Cheryl, you are in for a treat. There is food, of course, and some of these items we only have at weddings."

"Like what?"

"Wedding potatoes," Naomi cut in.

So she'd been listening after all, Cheryl thought to herself with a smirk.

"What type of potatoes are wedding potatoes?" she asked.

Levi lifted an eyebrow and looked to his maam, as if saying, *Okay, you butt in, so now you tell her.*

"They have potatoes, cream cheese, sour cream, butter, and American cheese. You mix them together, like in a casserole. Seth and I had them at our wedding too, and they are delicious."

Cheryl chuckled. "How could you go wrong with those ingredients?"

"Of course, Levi also likes the date pudding. Remind me next week, and I will get you recipes for both. I am sure Levi wouldn't mind being a taste tester…"

Cheryl nodded. Even though she wasn't sure when she'd be cooking for Levi, she had to admit she liked the idea of him hovering around, waiting to taste her creations.

"There will be music too," Levi said, getting back to her original question. "You will enjoy this because they will be singing in English this time—not in German."

"So I might be able to understand some of the words?"

"Ja."

"Any songs I know?"

"There is one called 'A Beautiful Wedded Life.' I cannot remember all the words, but one part says, 'As you now begin your wedded life together, may your wedded life be like the blooming roses.'"

"Oh." She puckered her lips. "I like the sound of that. It's beautiful."

Levi snickered and then looked away.

"What?" She softly punched his arm. "What's so funny?"

He leaned closer to her. "Do you want to know the truth?"

"Yes, of course."

"I know that when everyone thinks of blooming roses they think of the beauty, the colors, and the aroma...but I have picked enough roses from Maam's rose bushes to know there are plenty of thorns."

"Yes, I was thinking about that earlier. There will be bad times along with the good—for this couple and every other one. That's what happens when you put two people together."

Levi patted her hand "Ja, but today let us just think about the *goot*. And enjoy the rest."

He continued on, telling her about the gifts the bride and groom would offer to their attendants and the noisy interruption by school friends—which involved hammering trash can lids and other loud noises just for fun.

As she listened, the attendants began serving food to the tables. It was fascinating to watch and an honor to be included.

Silence fell as they watched table after table being served. Cheryl's stomach rumbled again. She patted it, knowing their food would be served soon enough.

Cheryl leaned into his shoulder, enough to connect. He leaned a little closer, and she enjoyed the contact, the joy of being with him—even if this was all she ever had.

Her mother's text flashed in her mind.

Did she really want to give up on whatever she had with Levi? Or maybe she should just face the facts that they came from two different worlds—two worlds that were impossible to mix.

It was too much to think about right now. She took all the feelings that simmered inside and tucked them in her heart, as if locking them away in a box. She would not let the questions ruin this moment.

The bride and groom moved to a table across from theirs, greeting each person at the table. "They look so content."

Levi nodded. "They should. They have known each other since they were children. Many of us have known they would marry for years. It was simply a matter of getting the finances they needed so they could have their own home."

"I wasn't sure what to get for them, especially since I didn't want to buy anything from the Swiss Miss. I decided every married couple needs to fill a pantry, so I bought them a basket of cheeses from Heini's."

Eli guffawed, and Levi muffled a chuckle. She looked in confusion between the brothers. Had she managed to offend with the gift? "What did I do?"

Levi cleared his throat then turned to her, merriment dancing in his eyes and reflecting in his raised cheeks. "Maybe you did not hear, Ezekiel's father, Alvin Byler, was a cheese maker. At Heini's."

Cheryl dropped her head in her hands and slumped over as the realization hit her. "Oh no. Tell me I didn't give cheese to the son of a cheese maker. Someone mentioned that at the ceremony, but I was so busy trying to understand what was happening it didn't really sink in." Heat climbed into her cheeks. "This is so embarrassing. I bought the son and daughter-in-law of a cheese maker the very cheese he makes!"

"It is better than buying it from the competition," Levi quipped.

"This is terrible."

Eli laughed harder and shared Cheryl's mistake with the others at the table, who soon joined in.

Finally, when the laughter died down, she lifted her head and fanned her face. "I hope Rhoda and Ezekiel think it's funny too. I just hope they don't tell too many people."

More laughter erupted around the table, and Cheryl wondered what she'd said now.

"Oh, that is another thing. One other part of this reception will be a time when the couple opens presents in front of all of the guests."

Cheryl's mouth gaped. "All of the guests?" She squared her shoulders. "Well, it's a good thing that I left my gift in the car. I might just let it stay there."

"Oh, do not be silly. I think everyone will love it. Your gift is sure to be a hit. In fact, I think Alvin will appreciate it. It has been a hard few days, and it will bring a smile to the cheese maker's face."

Cheryl nibbled on her lower lip. "Do you think so?"

"Ja, I will introduce you to Alvin after the meal. You will see that it doesn't matter to him—to them. A thoughtful gift is still thought filled regardless of where it originates."

His words soothed. Maybe the gift wasn't as improper as she feared. The last thing she wanted to do was insult her friend. "Thank you, Levi. I often feel like I'm still navigating through a fog."

"You are doing fine."

She tried to embrace his words, but this reinforced why any thought of a long-term relationship with Levi was out of the question. This couldn't work. She'd invariably embarrass him with her lack of knowledge about Amish ways. She could try. She could do her best to learn Amish ways, but it wasn't enough to keep from shining a glaring light on her lack of knowledge. She pasted a brave smile on and prayed Levi couldn't see through her.

Soon the attendants served food to their table, and after a silent prayer they began to eat. Cheryl dug into the potatoes first and then the date pudding. Both were delightful.

"So what do you think?" Naomi asked.

"Yes, I'd love the recipes, please. But if I make these, I'm not sure I'd share."

"Hey!" Levi piped up.

They continued eating, and again Cheryl's mind volleyed back and forth between hope and resolve. Hope that someday she and Levi could have a chance to grow their relationship, and resolve that a relationship between them would never happen and that she just had to move on.

After they finished eating, the attendants started handing out pie next. As delicious as it looked, Cheryl wasn't sure she'd be able to eat another bite.

As she looked around, Levi grabbed her hand. "You have been too quiet. I know what will take care of that." He stood and then tugged her to her feet. "Come with me."

She stood and adjusted her skirt before following him. "Where are we going?"

"I want to introduce you to Alvin Byler. I bet he can help you understand those cultures that you were researching."

Mr. Byler was a short, thin man. Salt and pepper colored his beard. He stood as Levi approached, curiosity on his face. "Good day, Levi."

"Mr. Byler. I would like to introduce my friend Cheryl Cooper. She is the manager of the Swiss Miss. Cheryl, this is the groom's father, Mr. Byler."

"It's a pleasure to meet you, sir."

"You may call me Alvin." He shook her hand then stroked his beard as he studied her. "I had heard you were in town, but I have not been over to Sugarcreek for months. I've heard good things about how welcoming you have been to Rhoda and others."

"Thank you."

Levi smiled down at Cheryl. "She is doing a great job with Mitzi's shop."

"Is your aunt enjoying her time in Papua New Guinea?"

What a quaint way to phrase it. "She's enjoying serving the Lord there, though it has presented its challenges. I'm glad to help her in this small way."

Levi slipped his arm closer to hers, and she felt settled in a way that felt so new and right.

"Levi tells me you are a cheese maker."

"You are misinformed. I am merely a worker. Others coax greatness from the ingredients. I merely replicate their recipes."

"Oh." A wave of disappointment washed over Cheryl, except perhaps that was the man's humility speaking. He might still be able to help her understand the process. "I've started looking into cheese making and am amazed by all the different varieties. I've always enjoyed cheese, but realize I've taken the process for granted. It's so complex."

"Not as complex as you believe. Think of cheese as children from the same parents. It is the same gene pool, but each child has different characteristics." His face had lit from within as he discussed the process. But then a cloud settled on his face. "That is the way it is with Heini's cheese...or rather *was* with our cheese."

"Aren't you upset about losing the cultures?" she asked.

"Burdened, yes. Upset? No. My parents taught me to respond, not to react." He sighed. "I will admit some days that is easier to do than others." He shrugged his shoulders as if dislodging a burden. "I hear the authorities think it might be arson. I am praying for the man who did this."

"You mean *whoever* did this?" Levi asked.

"Ne." He shook his head. "I know who it is. Teddy Harris is a local cheese maker. He has been a competitor to Heini's cheese factory for years. He came in the day before the fire, and he did not look happy."

"Why?" Cheryl leaned closer to him, hoping he would know something that would help unravel what had happened to cause such a tragedy.

Alvin nodded. "There has been bad blood since the time the current owner's father fired Teddy's father. Teddy has been determined to beat Heini's and prove that the superior cheese is his. Unfortunately, the awards speak in favor of Heini's. We are more creative and committed to excellence. Teddy has always looked for the easy path, the shortcut. Cheese does not allow that."

"My research taught me that cheese making is a delicate process."

"Incredibly so." Mr. Byler sighed again. "That is why the arson is such a tragedy. Buildings, equipment... they can be cleaned and replaced. Cultures are irreplaceable."

CHAPTER NINE

Cheryl and Levi walked back to the table where his family waited. She forced a smile at the sight of the friends whom she cared for, yet she couldn't shake a sense of deep sadness.

"Do you think he's right, Levi?"

"About Teddy?" Levi's voice sounded troubled. "I have known the family my whole life, though Teddy is older than me." He shrugged. "I do not know."

"It's hard to imagine someone doing something like that on purpose, but I suppose people act out of revenge all the time."

When they reclaimed their seats on the bench, Naomi looked at Cheryl. Concern caused her eyes to narrow and her eyebrows to fold. "Are you all right?"

"I am." The moment she spoke the half-truth, a nagging ache circled in her chest and settled in deep. "I guess I'm still burdened by the fire at Heini's. Levi introduced me to Mr. Byler, and talking to him made it very real all over again."

Naomi smiled sympathetically and then reached across the table and placed her hand on top of Cheryl's. "Your compassionate nature is a gift, but you cannot carry others' burdens for them. Not if you do so in a way that only transfers that burden to you." She squeezed Cheryl's hand and then let go. "Help others. Care for them. But ultimately trust them to *Gotte's* care. It is the only way to have peace deep down where it matters."

Cheryl let her friend's words soak in, like summer rains on parched ground. "When did you gain such wisdom?"

"It has taken a lifetime. And I still have much to learn."

Cheryl nodded. "Life is an ever-evolving journey, isn't it?"

"Yes, let it always lead you closer to our Father."

Cheryl let Naomi's words circle in her mind through the rest of the reception. *Will I ever get this right—this balance of caring for others yet not letting my heart get trampled every time there's tragedy?* Cheryl hoped so. Maybe she was more like her mom than she thought. Her mother was always thinking about—and praying for—the heavy burdens of this world. As a child Cheryl often found her in the mornings at the kitchen table reading her Bible and praying over a notebook full of prayer needs. Maybe she shouldn't cast away her mother's ideas so quickly or easily.

Minutes slipped into hours as she sat with the others and enjoyed the singing of wedding songs and the opening of gifts. She only blushed slightly when the couple opened her gift that Levi had retrieved from her car. Instead of those in attendance teasing her that the cheese maker's son had received cheese as a gift, everyone seemed touched by the gesture. To the bride and groom, Cheryl's present symbolized the gift that Heini's had been to the community for so many years.

As another round of singing began, Cheryl glanced at her watch and startled. "Oh my. I didn't realize it had gotten this late! I need to go give my congratulations to the couple and then head to the Swiss Miss. Lydia has graciously been watching the store by herself, but it's not fair to leave her by herself all day. I should at least go and help her with closing."

Esther stood. "Should I come with you? Together we can help Lydia with anything that she could not do."

"That would be great."

They gathered their coats and were saying good-bye to Mr. and Mrs. Byler at the door when someone knocked. Mr. Byler glanced around the room. "Who could it be? Everyone is here."

"Open the door, Husband, and we will see who is not." Several standing close to them chuckled at his wife's witty reply.

Mr. Byler opened the door, and Cheryl watched the color drain from his face. "Chief Twitchell?"

"I'm sorry to interrupt these proceedings, but I have a search warrant for your shop."

Any color left in the man's face disappeared as he stared at the chief. "I do not understand."

While Chief Twitchell often reminded Cheryl of the man who played the scarecrow in the *Wizard of Oz* movie, the Sugarcreek police chief was more solemn than she'd seen him in a while as he stood in the doorway. "Will you let me in, Alvin?" The chief pointed to refrigerated storage that Alvin had at the far end of the shop.

"I do not know if I should. I do not understand what is happening."

Cheryl stepped forward. "What is this about, Chief? This is his son's wedding."

"I know, and I'm very sorry. Unfortunately, I don't get to choose when I investigate. A judge gave me a search warrant to search your house and shop for the cultures from Heini's. I understand those are the only two places on your property that have refrigerated storage. Everyone needs to step outside of both buildings. Leave everything as it is. My officer outside will ask a few questions."

Alvin looked to his guests and then to the chief. "Chief, there must be three hundred people here and some of them are elderly. You can't mean they all have to go outside?"

"Actually I do. Yesterday, Alvin, you asked me what I was doing to find the people who started the fire. Well, this is part of it." The chief turned to the crowd of curious onlookers. The music had stopped, and everyone's attention was now focused on the scene at the door. Chief Twitchell lifted his hands and addressed them. "Now, folks, if you could all kindly make your way outside. I will make this as quick as I can. Either I'll find what I'm lookin' for, or it won't be here. Easy enough."

Cheryl fought the urge to roll her eyes. Of course those were the two outcomes. Still, she didn't understand why he was here now, interrupting the festivities. "What exactly are you looking for?" she dared to ask.

"It's all in the search warrant." Chief Twitchell handed it to Mr. Byler. "Alvin, you and your wife may stay inside, but you will need to be where I can see you while also stayin' out of my way."

His face fell. "I do not understand." The tremor in his voice caused Cheryl's heart to ache.

"Here, Mr. Byler. Let me see the warrant." Cheryl wasn't an attorney, but maybe she could help.

The Millers had put on their coats and were headed to the door. Naomi slowed as she neared Cheryl. "We will take Esther to the Swiss Miss. You stay and help the Bylers."

"Thank you." Cheryl gave her friend a quick hug then opened the warrant. What she read shocked her. The information said that the police had reason to believe that the cultures were being stored in Mr. Byler's shop or home. "Some of the cultures survived the fire?"

Chief Twitchell turned to her with a sigh. "Cheryl, the cultures weren't in the fire. They were removed before it started."

"So the fire was set to cover the theft?"

"Maybe."

Officer Anderson hurried in. "Spencer cleared the home too and has the others corralled. What do you want me to do?"

"Let's start with the refrigerators. This warrant is pretty limited. We have permission to search in likely places the cultures would be stored. After talkin' to Lisa Troyer, I understand they have to be refrigerated. If the temperature isn't regulated, then the cultures might as well have been in the fire." Chief Twitchell turned to Mr. Byler. "I'd like to make this as easy and noninvasive on you and your family as possible. However, I will search for those cultures. Would you like to tell me where you refrigerate things?"

"We have a refrigerator here in the shop and also a small gas refrigerator in the kitchen. Those are the only two locations."

"Take me to your kitchen first."

Since she wasn't told to stay in the shop, Cheryl followed the men to the kitchen in the house. What should be the warm and welcoming part of the home was absolutely chaotic. It was an explosion of covered dishes, trays loaded with cheese, meat, and rolls of all kinds, yet all unquestionably homemade. It appeared that whoever had been in the kitchen was preparing more food for the guests who still remained. And this was after they'd already finished off tables full of food from lunch. She could only imagine the bounty that had loaded every surface before the wedding.

"There's the kitchen refrigerator." Mr. Byler pointed to the gas-powered appliance. It no longer surprised Cheryl to find modern conveniences in the Amish homes around Sugarcreek.

"Thank you. Now if you will step away." Chief Twitchell pulled on a pair of gloves, opened the door, and then began a thorough examination of the contents. As the minutes ticked away, he meticulously removed one container at a time, opening them to check the contents. The refrigerator was packed with more items for the wedding, and checking each container was time-consuming. Cheryl bit the inside of her mouth to resist the urge to help. Without a doubt, he would not welcome her assistance and was more likely to call it interference than help.

Chief Twitchell opened a small five-by-eight-inch container with a red lid and then froze. He pulled out his phone to take a picture of it then set the container to the side as he typed in a message. After that he dialed a number. "Lisa, Chief Twitchell. I texted you a photo. Can you verify that this is cheese culture?"

Cheryl couldn't hear what Lisa said, but her heart sank as the chief started nodding.

"Good. Does this look like all of it?" He paused and then nodded again. "I'll keep looking." Then he dialed another number. "Spencer, any trouble out there with the weddin' guests?" Another pause. "Then get in here. I need help processin' evidence."

Mr. Byler swayed next to her. "I do not know how it got there."

Chief Twitchell shoved his phone into his pocket. "All I know right now is one of the cultures was found in your refrigerator. Now, Lisa tells me that's not all of them, so I'm going to keep diggin' through this fridge." He turned to Alvin. "Do you have any other refrigerators? Anywhere on this farm? The barn? The cellar? Other outbuildings?"

Mr. Byler shook his head. "Ne. The one in the shop and this one are the only two."

When the officer hustled into the kitchen a few minutes later, Chief Twitchell pointed at the pile of containers on the floor next to him. "Put on some gloves and go back through these. Make sure I didn't miss anything that looks like cheese cultures."

"What do those look like?"

The chief pointed at Byler. "Ask him."

Cheryl relaxed as Levi slid into the room next to her.

"How is it going?" he whispered.

Cheryl slid closer until she could feel the heat from his arm. "Not well. I'm worried for Mr. Byler."

Byler continued to maintain his innocence as he surveyed the containers Officer Spencer was going through. "Many of these containers are not ours. They were brought by wedding guests to help my wife and bless my son and his new wife. Must this be done now?"

Chief Twitchell sat back on his haunches and surveyed the inside shelves of the fridge. "I've been through them all. I only see the one container."

"He says these four also contain the cultures." The officer waved at Byler then at a stack of small containers.

"Good. Go check the shop's refrigerator too then let me know if you find any." Cheryl couldn't believe anyone would think Mr. Byler had taken the cultures. If he had, why would he have left them in his refrigerator? It made more sense that someone planted them in the midst of the wedding chaos.

The kitchen grew silent after the deputy hurried out. Alvin leaned against the kitchen table, his hair rumpled and his beard looking unkempt from all the times he'd tugged and pulled at them. "Chief, there are hundreds of people here. Any one of them could have planted the cultures."

The chief rubbed his nose as he studied the Amish man. "That *is* a problem." Cheryl grew nervous as he continued to stare at Mr. Byler. "But why would anyone else steal it? And how would they know it needs to be refrigerated?"

"Why would Alvin?" That question had bothered Cheryl all during the search.

"Maybe because he tried to buy the business from Lisa's family. They turned him down, according to my sources."

Alvin held his hands up in front of him as if warding off a threat. "I only made the offer to help them out. There are many cheese makers in the area. Many others would understand cultures and how to care for them."

Levi looked from man to man. "Chief, you really think Mr. Byler stole the cultures to start his own business?"

"It's as good of a motive as any we have right now." The chief gestured toward the pile of five containers. "And he has the cultures."

"There have to be other motives too. Like their value," Cheryl said. "Those in the cheese-making industry know how valuable those cultures are. The Heini factory has won numerous awards."

"Or someone could want to hurt a lot of people." Levi's comment startled Cheryl.

"What do you mean?"

"I know a lot of farmers in this area, and many of them provide milk for Heini's. All their milk comes from Amish farms and without the cultures..."

"Without the cultures there is no cheese production." Cheryl's eyes widened at the implications. "Without the cheese, there's no need for that milk. This is going to greatly impact our community in the worst way."

"And at Christmas too."

CHAPTER TEN

Cheryl walked into her home after a long day at the wedding, and both sadness and joy fought for a front-row seat. She'd been both sad and startled by the discovery of the cultures in Alvin's refrigerator. He surely wasn't involved, was he? It seemed to her someone must have taken advantage of the wedding chaos to plant them. But if so, who would do it and why?

Mixed with that were the peaceful images of the wedding. Would she ever have that? Maybe her mom was right. If she didn't do something, she'd never have her happily ever after. A moment of looking into her love's eyes and pledging her forever to him.

Reality? She wasn't getting any younger. While she may have grimaced when her mom mentioned her ticking biological clock, Momma spoke truth.

She glanced at her laptop. She needed to get to the shop and help Lydia with closing, but would it hurt to take a few minutes to open the Web site and see what it offered?

No, I'll wait. I can't do that to Lydia. During the Christmas season the Swiss Miss was busy with customers looking for the perfect gift. Lydia had graciously tended the shop all day, but now Cheryl needed to get in and help the young woman.

The Web site would still be there when she got back home or even over the weekend. Cheryl quickly changed, petted Beau and gave him fresh water, and then slipped on her jacket.

She stepped outside, and the cold wind nipped her nose. With it came the chilling memory of Mr. Byler being escorted through the crowded guests shivering on his porch to the waiting police car. Chief Twitchell had said it was only for questioning, but Cheryl knew it could quickly spiral into something worse. Mrs. Byler had been almost inconsolable until several of the guests stepped forward and took her inside.

Although part of Cheryl wanted to stay, her presence wouldn't calm Mrs. Byler. At the Swiss Miss she could at least bring order to the shelves and displays. *I wish I could do more though.*

Cheryl simply couldn't see Mr. Byler as the thief. True, she hadn't met him before that morning, but it did seem awfully convenient that the cultures had appeared in his fridge on a day so many people were in and out of his home celebrating the wedding. It would be easy for someone to slip in and add the items without anyone really noticing. Cheryl wished she could have asked the other guests if they'd seen anything out of the ordinary. Maybe Naomi could help her with that throughout the coming days.

Cheryl arrived nearly at closing time with Beau in his carrier. Lydia always complained if Cheryl didn't show up with her furry friend. Lydia was building a beautiful Christmas display with handcrafted ornaments. Somehow the Christmas spirit seemed a long ways away when her friends at Heini's and now Mr. Byler were embroiled in this mess, both in such different ways.

Seth had taken Naomi home, but Esther had stayed to help restock the shelves. Cheryl settled on a chair behind the cash register, trying to figure out what still needed to be done before closing.

Esther carried seven new wall quilts to her. "These arrived while you were out. I entered them into the inventory. Is it okay to display them?"

Cheryl nodded as she quickly flipped through the stack. "These are beautiful."

"Ja. Three were quilted by Almina Troyer, Lydia's mom, and the others by Joanna Troyer."

"I'll be sure to tell the ladies how much I appreciate their work. These should sell by Christmas." Cheryl helped Esther refold them for display. Embroidered script on one caught her attention.

If you had never tasted the bitter, you would not know what is sweet.

The words resonated in her soul.

Many of her friends were going through hard, bitter trials. The kinds of trials that were so hard to see God in the midst of. Yet those hard times made the good times so much sweeter. If all people ever experienced were joy and peace, then those emotions would eventually lose their power and become routine. In fact the words sounded a lot like a recent letter she had received from Aunt Mitzi.

Cheryl pulled it from her apron pocket as she headed back to the office. She eagerly anticipated her missionary aunt's letters because the woman walked with such wisdom. Now as she reread the letter, the wisdom echoed that of the words on the lap quilt.

Dearest Cheryl,

It's hard to believe the seasons have changed again in Sugarcreek when the weather remains hot and humid here day after day. The only difference is some days feel like a sauna and other days feel like I'm drinking hot water when I breathe. Mind you, I'm not complaining, just acknowledging the reality.

My mission work is easier now. Not in the actual labor, but in the knowing what to expect. The people accept me. The work is valuable. But I think there's also great peace in knowing that God has placed me exactly where He wants me. The bad days make the good ones that much better. And the good days make the bad days endurable.

Don't worry about me though. All is well. God continues to grant me His grace for each task that is placed before me. I count it an honor to serve Him and the natives here.

Know that I love you and will try to get on Skype and connect again soon. Electricity is still one of the intermittent conveniences out here. I'd better sign off since I hear the call that the canoe is about ready to leave.

Much love,
Aunt Mitzi

Cheryl refolded the letter and tucked it back into her apron pocket. The words swirled through her mind as she answered Lydia's call to help a customer.

It was after dark when Cheryl returned home and released Beau from his carrier. He shook himself with a shiver and then pranced straight to his kitty bed. He wove around a couple of times and then settled in, ready to take another long nap. The idea sounded really good. Curl up with a blanket and a novel on Aunt Mitzi's cozy couch. Maybe she'd do that after she grabbed a bit of supper.

She was preparing a Cobb salad with all the fixings when her phone dinged that a text had come in. She glanced at the screen and then sighed when she saw it was from her mom. She imagined what it would say even before she read it.

Cheryl closed her eyes. "Have you looked at the Web site?"

Then she opened them and read the text. Still waiting to hear what you think of e-Love. Very excited to see you try it out.

Yep.

Exactly what she'd expected.

She hated the way her reaction to the text made her feel. Mom meant well. She really did, and Cheryl needed to respond like an adult rather than a hormonal teenager. Ignoring her mother wouldn't make her—or the e-Love site—go away.

Cheryl ate her salad and then faced the inevitable. The only way to get her mom to quit asking about e-Love was to try it. She grabbed her laptop then sat on the couch and adjusted a couple of throw pillows behind her back. This could take a while. As she shifted back and forth and scrunched into a comfortable position, Beau hopped on to the couch. He watched her as if trying to decide if this was some new game he was supposed to play with her. After a moment, he settled down and placed his head on her arm so he could monitor everything she typed.

"Might as well get this over with." She plunked in the e-Love address then entered the log-in information her mom had sent her.

"Last thing I need is Mom expressing interest for me... Oh, Momma, what will you think of next?" She shuddered at the thought, and Beau lifted his head indignantly. He suffered to look at her then stood and stretched each leg out to its full length before leaping off the edge of the couch and disappearing in the direction of his food dish.

"Some moral support you are, Beau, leaving me to do this by myself." She groaned and then screwed her face up. "I have to get this over with. That's all."

When she looked at her profile, she was surprised to see that her mom had filled in some of it for her. As she reviewed the answers, Cheryl had to admit they were worded like she had written them. The photo was at least ten years old. She grinned, knowing that old photo wouldn't get any attention. She considered changing it to a photo more accurate of what she looked like today but didn't bother. It wasn't as if she were going to take any of this seriously. Still, she'd poke around to see what this was about. Momma had signed her up for three months. That should be plenty of time to see if she liked the site and its process.

As she looked at the requests that had come in, Cheryl compared each picture to Levi. Did this feel like a betrayal of him? Yes, it did in some ways. At the same time, Levi had made no promises to her. Their future was far from set. Maybe the best way to know if Levi was the man for her was to explore whether there were other men who could catch her attention the way he had.

She didn't want to think about another man capturing her heart.

She simply couldn't go that far right now.

Purposefully, she scanned the profiles of guys from around Sugarcreek. Many of them looked to be nice men, but they simply didn't capture her attention. Still, she kept scrolling and reading the short bios. She tried not to pay too much attention to each man's appearance. Who knew if their photos were as dated as the one Momma had posted of her?

She had nearly reached the end of the first page when one of the profiles made her stop. This one was a businessman in Sugarcreek. He only gave his first name: Elliott, which wasn't a name she recognized. His picture was handsome enough. His bio shared that he attended one of the local churches and that he liked to travel for both pleasure and short-term missions trips. One intriguing tidbit was that he went to Europe each Christmas to visit family. She tried to imagine a life that allowed for that kind of travel. It sounded magical.

Maybe she should send him a note, suggest that they meet for coffee at the Honey Bee. That would be innocent enough and a way to see if he was anything like his profile.

Her hands froze above the keys.

Part of her wanted to reach out to him, see what was possible. But a bigger part of her couldn't. It didn't feel right, not yet.

Instead, she printed his profile. She'd pray about it and see how she felt in another day or two.

Maybe then it wouldn't feel like a betrayal of Levi.

Chapter Eleven

Morning light filtered through the bedroom curtains as Cheryl stretched. She glanced at her bedside clock and frowned.

It was eight fifteen, and her alarm was set to go off at seven thirty. What? Had she bumped it and turned it off during the night? She'd need to hurry if she wanted to get to the shop in time to get everything set up for the Vogel brothers. She hadn't seen them much this week, which meant they were probably planning their regular checkers game for today.

As she threw back the covers trying to force herself out of bed, a soft ding sounded from somewhere down the hall, followed a moment later by another ding. While the sound was muted, depending on how long it had been recurring, that might have been what woke her up. That and Beau tap-dancing across her stomach as she lay in bed getting her bearings. At the edge of the bed, the Siamese cat stopped and looked over his shoulder at her.

His message was clear: "Time to get up, Sleepyhead. My stomach requires sustenance."

She reached forward to rub him behind the ears, but he hopped off the bed then waited as if to make sure she actually crawled out from under her warm covers.

The thought of rolling over and ignoring the cat and electronic nuisance tempted Cheryl. It would be wonderful to get even another half hour of rest. But as the sound kept alerting, she knew she wouldn't be able to sleep until she figured out its source. Plus she needed to be a responsible adult and open the Swiss Miss.

She grabbed her cell phone from where it was charging on her nightstand and clicked to double check the time. An alert reminded her Aunt Mitzi was going to Skype her fifteen minutes earlier. "Oh no! I hope she's still waiting."

Cheryl threw on a robe and hurried down the hallway to the living room. She ran her fingers through her hair and prayed it didn't look as bad as she feared. She didn't want to miss this chance to connect with her aunt. Letters were nice, but Skype calls were so much better. Watching Aunt Mitzi as she talked told Cheryl so much more than the words did. Aunt Mitzi had never been great at hiding her emotions. Instead, she tended to wear them on her sleeves for all to see. It was part of her charm.

When Cheryl picked up her laptop and plopped it in her lap, she was relieved to see that the call was still waiting. She hurriedly pressed the sequence of buttons to log in and then waited for her aunt's grainy image to appear. Her gray hair remained short and spiky, almost as spunky as she was. Cheryl couldn't imagine launching such an adventure in her mid-sixties, but her aunt thrived wherever she was.

"Aunt Mitzi, I am so sorry."

"Don't worry, Cheryl." Mitzi grinned at her. "You're still my favorite niece."

Cheryl chuckled. "I'm your only niece."

"And I love you for it." She seemed to study Cheryl. "Rough night?"

"Not the easiest. A couple days ago there was a fire at Heini's."

"That's terrible. Is everyone okay?"

"Physically, yes. I don't know about financially though. Someone set the fire to cover up the theft of the cheese cultures. Without those, Heini's can't make their unique cheese."

Aunt Mitzi nodded. "Cheese making is such a delicate process. I've tried my hand at it here thanks to Georgie. I've always thought goat's milk makes fantastic cheese, but it's definitely not as simple as the pros make it look. I can't seem to get the cultures right."

"I had no idea how vulnerable they were or how important to the cheese-making process." Cheryl sighed. "But that's not the worst of it."

"Is trouble following you around, kiddo? It seems to like to find you."

"Torment me, you mean." Cheryl leaned closer to the Web camera, really glad that Aunt Mitzi couldn't smell her morning breath.

"Something like that. So tell me. What else is going on?"

"Chief Twitchell and a couple of his deputies crashed the Byler wedding yesterday. They disrupted the reception and then took Alvin Byler in for questioning. Do you know him?"

Aunt Mitzi glanced away and thought for a minute. "He's been into the Swiss Miss a few times with his wife, but I don't know the Bylers as well as I do the Millers and others. His wife would sell me jams and jellies, occasionally cheese, and I heard his daughter is a wonderful quilter."

"His new daughter-in-law, Rhoda, brought me several wall quilts to sell this year. They are beautiful and selling so well. I'm glad because the wedding I attended yesterday was hers." Cheryl fiddled with her robe's belt. "I hate that her special day was marred by a police search and then her father-in-law being hauled off to jail in front of everyone."

"Umm. Definitely not what she would have ordered, but God will be with her."

"I know. It's just that this tragedy reaches to so many different families. Levi was telling me about all the families who sell their milk to Heini's. If Heini's isn't making cheese because of the stolen cultures and destroyed factory, how will all those families earn a living? And to have this happen at Christmastime? It seems cruel."

"The Lord promised that in this world we would have trouble but that He has overcome the world. There is such encouragement in that. And this will only be for a season. Heini's will rebuild. I can almost guarantee it. With all that stainless steel, I bet there's a lot to salvage." Aunt Mitzi smiled softly as she looked at Cheryl. "Maybe there is something you can do to testify to one of those families who is affected in this hard time, sharing the great love of God. Imagine the impact any small act of kindness would have on them and their families."

"Their needs must be massive."

"Maybe, but maybe some families saved for a rainy day like this. Think instead of one area where you can provide a real impact that makes a difference."

"Food?"

"Sure, but anyone can do that, and I bet their community will reach out in that way." Mitzi studied her with a loving expression. "What about providing something they'll all need that isn't necessarily in a budget."

"I'm sure some of them have children."

Mitzi nodded with a gentle smile. "Most of them will. So what if you provided Christmas gifts for a few of the kids whose parents no longer have a place to sell their milk? You won't need to do it alone, but providing that for the children at Christmas will be a huge blessing for those families."

The idea caught fire within Cheryl's spirit. "What about dolls from the Sugarcreek Sisters Quilt Shoppe? And wooden toys from Jacob Hoffman's store? And books from By His Grace?"

"Ezra might have some things at the Old Amish Store as well."

Mitzi and Cheryl spent another fifteen minutes brainstorming gifts and chatting.

Cheryl smiled at her aunt's enthusiasm. "Thank you. This is a great idea that could make a real difference for some of the families."

"I know you, Cheryl. You like to show your love by doing. This is a great way to do exactly that."

"I have to admit it's daunting. There are so many families."

"Pray and ask God to show you the right families to help. He may not be calling you to help all of them. If you pray, He'll show you which are the right ones for you to serve."

The thought of helping some but not all broke Cheryl's heart. "And for the others?"

"God will take care of them. He may use a different tool to do so." Aunt Mitzi sighed. "I wish I'd learned this lesson when I was your age. I often thought I had to be the one to do all of it or it wouldn't happen. I've learned that's simply not true. In fact, I can get in the way of God using someone else when I believe I have to do it all."

Cheryl let the words sink in. There was the ring of truth to them. Maybe she needed to focus on the families God placed on her heart. She could organize a massive effort—she had the skills and passion, but maybe that wasn't what she was supposed to do this time. "I'll pray about it."

"Perfect." Mitzi's smile warmed Cheryl. "Did Levi mention whom he knew would be most affected?"

Cheryl listed a couple. "But I really didn't remember all the names he listed. I'm afraid they didn't stick."

"No problem. Let me tell you what I know about some of the dairy farmers. You wouldn't have a real need to know them since we don't sell raw milk." Mitzi was halfway through telling her about one family when the connection dropped.

Cheryl tried to reconnect. When it didn't happen, she let out a sigh and then sent up a quick prayer, thanking God for all of the time they had talked. The connection was so undependable, the time was a real gift.

Cheryl leaned back in her chair and glanced at the wall clock. She'd need to race if she was going to get to the Swiss Miss before the Vogel brothers. Part of her was a little horrified that Aunt Mitzi had seen her in such a state, but that was the wonderful thing about knowing someone loved you unconditionally. She didn't need to worry that Aunt Mitzi's love would be changed one iota because of how she looked. Now the brothers might not appreciate her showing up in her bathrobe with spiky hair flying in all directions, but Aunt Mitzi didn't mind.

As she raced to the shower, Cheryl grabbed a notepad and jotted down her list of possible gifts for children. Then she paused. Maybe she should check with Naomi and confirm who the affected families were and whether they would welcome this kind of help. The last thing she wanted to do was embarrass anyone, but she'd seen the community come together so many times to help others it would be wonderful to do the same for them.

Aunt Mitzi was right though. She'd need to pray and ask God for confirmation that this was what He wanted her to do and ask Him to lead her to the right families that most needed the help. In fact, she'd take time to do that as she drove to the shop.

CHAPTER TWELVE

The Vogel brothers stood outside the Swiss Miss as Cheryl walked up. Ben made a show of stomping his feet and shivering while Rueben reached for Beau's carrier.

"Let me take that for you, Cheryl."

"Thanks, Rueben." Cheryl gratefully handed him Beau and then pulled her keys from her coat's deep pocket. "Sorry to keep you waiting. Aunt Mitzi Skyped this morning."

"We have not been here long despite Ben's show over there."

Ben rolled his eyes and grinned at his younger brother. "Thanks for ruining all my fun."

Cheryl turned the key and then opened it, and then Ben grabbed the door.

"But it will feel good to get inside," he said.

Cheryl knew her cheeks had to be rosy from the bite of the wind. "I'll get the coffeepot on in a minute."

The men settled in at the checkerboard. Cheryl let Beau out of his cage, deposited it in the office under the desk, and he took off while she hung up her coat. Fifteen minutes later she had the shop swept and ready to unlock the door for the local customers who could come before the Swiss Miss officially opened. It was such a charming local tradition that the shops up and down Main Street and around the square had special hours in the morning for local residents.

Her Amish helpers would arrive before the tourist buses, but for now she could handle the flow of the shop on her own. She turned on the Christmas music, and peace settled over her. A soft smile touched her lips as she sat at the stool behind the wide wooden counter and assessed the store without the extra distractions. It looked like some of the candy in the counter's display case needed to be refilled. A great task for Lydia or Esther when they arrived.

The phone rang, and Cheryl quickly picked it up. "Thank you for calling the Swiss Miss. How can I help you?"

"Hi. Is this Cheryl?" The familiar voice made Cheryl smile.

"Kinsley?"

"Yes, ma'am. I wondered if you needed any help this Christmas season. I liked working for you last year, and, well, I could use the money if you need me."

Cheryl thought about it. The Christmas season was going well, but if she decided to really help some of the families hurt by the fire, she'd be out of the shop more. That meant she'd be relying a lot on Lydia and Esther. "What hours are you available?"

"The same as last year if it works for you."

"It might. Why don't you give me your number, and I'll call after I check Esther's and Lydia's schedules."

"Thank you!"

Before long, the girls arrived and agreed that it could be helpful to have Kinsley return to the store for the season. Esther smiled knowingly at Cheryl. "You will get involved in helping others and be away. Kinsley will help us at those times."

"Thanks for understanding, girls." Esther was likely right. Cheryl would have a hard time not trying to find out who had hurt her friends at Heini's. She might not know the Bylers well, but she hated the thought that Mr. Byler had been set up for the theft of the cheese cultures. At the same time, maybe he had used the chaos of the wedding to hide the cultures in plain sight. "I'll see how flexible Kinsley is. Right now I need to work on orders. The tourists are cleaning us out of candles and wall quilts."

"Do not forget to check for lotions. The goat's milk lotions and soaps have been popular as bundled sets." Lydia smiled at Esther. "It was a great idea to tie them with that ribbon, Esther."

"Just something I saw on Pinterest." The young woman giggled and then waved a hand at Lydia who looked slightly shocked. "At the library. I figure if it was an idea to help here, it was a good use of the technology."

Cheryl laughed as she squeezed her friend's shoulder. "I'm glad you saw it. And I'll make note to check if we have more in stock."

"I think it is all on the floor." Lydia pointed to the display table. "I put all I could find out yesterday."

Cheryl spent the next hour checking the inventory and then calling her various suppliers and vendors to see who could get more items to her on short notice. There seemed to be more tourists than the prior Christmas season, and that one had kept her busy.

When she made it back into the shop, Lydia and Esther were both engaged with different women who were shopping for full-size quilts. If those sold, it would be a nice influx of cash for the store and mean that Cheryl could buy more. People often balked at the steep price tags, but when you realized the hundreds of hours of time that went into each beautiful creation, the prices were understandable.

Cheryl settled on the stool behind the counter and started refilling the candy bins. It wouldn't surprise her to see a group of school kids come in after school for a snack. Candy bags also made great stocking stuffers. Maybe she'd build on Esther's idea and prepackage some bags for quick, impulse buys. Set a small tower of them next to the cash register and customers might pick them up spur of the moment.

She smiled at the thought. She could pick up some cute Christmasy cellophane bags in addition to the traditional little white wax bags. It would look so cute. And maybe she could pick up actual ornaments to fill. That was an idea she had seen on Pinterest. It looked easy and would be fun. Cheryl had finished filling the last bin when Lydia brought a slim Amish woman to her.

"This is Jessica Mast. She wondered if she might have a moment of your time." Lydia's eyes begged Cheryl to give the woman her full attention.

"Of course." Cheryl brushed her hands on her apron and smiled at the woman. "How can I help you?"

The woman was about Cheryl's height but slightly stooped in the shoulders as if the basket she carried were weighed down by an assortment of cares. Her kapp covered hair that was brown with streaks of gray, and her soft gray eyes were weary. "I wondered if you might be willing to purchase some of these." She opened her basket's lid and pulled out a variety of colorful quilted pot holders. "I have thirty in here. They are all handmade by me from the leftover material from my quilts."

Cheryl reached for one. "May I?"

"Yes, ma'am." The woman watched her closely as Cheryl picked up a beautiful pot holder made from lavender and teal calico prints.

"The stitching on these is beautiful. These are almost too perfect to use."

"That is what my husband has said. He accused me of making artwork rather than something useful. I planned to give them as gifts...but..." She shrugged. "With the fire, my husband cannot sell his milk to Heini's, and that means we are taking a reduced price for it. Every little bit will help."

Cheryl flipped through the stack. The color combinations were beautiful and appealing. "I would be willing to take all thirty on consignment. We could start with a price of twenty-five dollars and see if that sells. Some people might think that is steep for a pot holder, but others will realize each of these is a beautiful piece of art." She turned to Lydia. "Don't you think some of the ladies who come in here could be encouraged to make a display by hanging a cluster together?"

"Yes, ma'am." Her eyes twinkled as she met Cheryl's gaze. "Some of the tourists would be delighted to have several authentic Amish pot holders."

"So does consignment work for you, Mrs. Mast?"

"Yes." The woman nodded her head enthusiastically. "That would be a true blessing from Gott. I was not sure how we would have the money for Christmas for our children."

"If we sell them at twenty-five dollars, I'll keep five dollars as the consignment fee and the rest will be yours. And any that don't sell, you can reclaim. Or if you change your mind, you can come get any that are still here at any time. How does that sound?"

"Wonderful." The woman set the basket on a nearby table and then reached for Cheryl's hands. She squeezed them as her eyes brightened. "*Danki*. This has added an extra burden to our family. I assured Myron that the Lord would provide, but I know sometimes we are to use our gifts and talents to provide the avenue for His help. You are an instrument of His today."

The words warmed Cheryl through. "Thank you for thinking of the Swiss Miss. Now let's see if we can sell them for you."

It only took a few minutes to complete the consignment form. As they worked on it, Cheryl asked how many children they had.

"Five. Two girls and three boys. All stair steps between one and nine."

"How wonderful, but you really have your hands full."

"I love every moment." As Lydia's eyebrows rose, Mrs. Mast laughed. "Most moments. Jedediah can be a handful."

Cheryl considered her conversation with Aunt Mitzi. She also considered her prayer on the drive here, *Lord, show me who to help.* Had the Lord answered so quickly? She saw that He had.

She took a deep breath and offered a soft smile. "I'm not sure how to ask this, but could I buy Christmas presents for them for you? To help your family at this time?"

The woman's mouth dropped open. Her eyes grew rounder, and Cheryl noted the smallest hint of tears. "I do not want to impose—because I know Gott will provide..."

"Maybe He wants to use me to do that...as a way to provide for them."

Tears slipped down the woman's cheeks. "I would be humbled to receive your gifts."

"Thank you." Answering tears swelled in her eyes. "Could you write their names and ages on this piece of paper? Maybe a note about what they like to do as well."

Mrs. Mast accepted the paper and pen that Cheryl handed her. "Please remember we celebrate Christmas on a smaller scale."

"I'll be sure to have Esther and Lydia help."

"We would love to do that," Esther said. She approached Cheryl with a smile.

When Mrs. Mast left a few minutes later, the woman looked much less burdened than when she'd arrived, and Cheryl had a new lightness to her heart.

"That was a kind thing to do, Cheryl. Danki." Lydia's smile seemed to light her entire face. "I would like to help purchase the Christmas gifts."

"Please don't feel like you need to. This was a small enough thing. I'll enjoy shopping for the children. I wasn't sure I could buy the pot holders outright, but consignment at this time of year could actually work better for her." Cheryl slipped the form into a folder. "I wish I could do more for her."

Lydia sighed. "You gave her hope. Maybe that is enough for today."

As Cheryl walked the folder with the consignment agreement and list of children to her office, she realized there was a lot of truth to Lydia's words. While the action might have seemed and felt small to her, to Mrs. Mast it had been enough. It had given her hope that God was providing in a way where there seemed to be no way. If He wanted to use Cheryl as part of that, then she was grateful and humbled. Maybe this was the confirmation she needed to pursue the idea Aunt Mitzi had given her. This was one Amish family she could help. As He brought more across her path, she could choose to help them as well.

Chapter Thirteen

The evening sky outside the Swiss Miss's heart-shaped window was turning dusky, sinking into velvety darkness when Cheryl flipped the sign to Closed. Esther and Lydia slid on their capes and scarves, giggling the whole time. As they approached the door, Esther stopped next to Cheryl.

"I will see you in an hour, right?"

Cheryl smiled at the young woman with the cheeky grin. "Yes, I won't be late for dinner. Tell your mom I should be there by six."

"All right. It looks like Lydia's father is here." The girls left with a flurry of waves and the swish of capes.

In the aftermath, Cheryl emptied the cash register and then put the day's proceeds into the safe. She would get the deposit ready in the morning. As Esther had reminded her, she had plans for a home-cooked meal surrounded by friends who were growing as close as family. Maybe someday they *would* be family.

She shook her head to clear the thought and then picked up Beau. She rubbed the Siamese under the chin, and he closed his eyes and began to purr. "It's been a good day, boy. First a chat with Aunt Mitzi and then the opportunity to help a family in need." She must have stopped rubbing because he nosed her hand.

Cheryl laughed and hugged him closer. "Come on, Beau. Let's get you home."

When Cheryl got home, she quickly changed into a soft powder-blue sweater and slipped on a pair of warm corduroy pants. She touched up her makeup with a light hand and a swipe of gloss before bundling back into her coat.

She paused to admire the Christmas tree as she pulled her coat on. Beau followed her to the door.

"Need something, boy?"

He meowed and turned to the kitchen with his tail high. She laughed and followed him then stopped when she realized his bowl was empty. "You are a hungry guy today."

After she refilled his food bowl and replaced his water, she grabbed her purse and headed to her car.

The drive was quiet, with a sense of peace settling over her as she left Sugarcreek behind and wound along the county roads past the corn maze and along the lovely creek that burbled brightly during the spring. Now it was quiet. Cheryl crossed the charming old-fashioned covered bridge that stretched over the creek. When she reached the other side, the Millers' large, white farmhouse with a wraparound porch sat waiting. Next to the house were the family's two buggies. The family's horses would either be inside the large fenced pasture or safe in the warm barn. She pulled her car near the buggies and parked.

Warm light spilled from the front windows, and a curtain in the window nearest to the door fluttered. As she climbed out of her car, the front door opened with the light silhouetting Levi's strong form. A soft smile spread on Cheryl's face.

She closed her car door and walked toward the porch steps. "Hello, Levi."

He stepped toward her and smiled. "I am glad you could join us tonight."

"You know I'd never miss a chance for one of your mom's home-cooked meals." At least not if she could help it. She'd gone through a small window of time when Cheryl's mom had told her she did too much and needed to scale back. During that time she'd declined an invitation or two before she realized time spent with this family actually fed her soul and built her up. She needed time with people like the Millers who loved her. Meals like this energized her in a way that time alone couldn't.

"Maam is ready for us to sit down." He grabbed her hand and helped her up the last step before gently squeezing her fingers and releasing her so he could open the door.

She followed him into the family's living area, and the aromas of food greeted her.

She breathed in deeply. "Something smells delicious."

He led her across the large and colorful rag rug that lay on the polished wood floor. A blue cloth couch sat against one wall, a lovely white lace doily across the back. Dark blue-and-white quilted pillows were positioned against the arms of the couch. Nearby were three beautifully carved wooden rocking chairs and two recliners. An evening fire crackled in the large brick fireplace pushing back against the December chill.

Then they walked into a room even larger than the living room. A buzz of conversation met them as they walked into the room, the clear heart of this house. A huge wooden table sat in the middle of the room. Dishes filled with wonderful food had been set out on the table for supper. Elizabeth and Naomi bustled around the stove and sink filling serving dishes with food while Seth and Eli carried on a conversation at one end of the table.

"Where's Esther?"

Levi groaned. "Delaying as long as possible. She seems to feel after working for you all day, she doesn't need to hurry down and help Maam. Today Maam is giving her grace."

Cheryl grimaced as Naomi turned. "I didn't realize Esther working for me could be a hardship here."

Naomi set the bowl she carried on the table then hurried over, a welcoming light in her eyes. "Nonsense. Do not listen to this son of mine." She patted Levi's arm. "He overexaggerates things at times. Esther had a headache. She will be down in a moment." Naomi turned to her other daughter. "Elizabeth, would you go tell her it is time?"

Elizabeth nodded and then slipped off her apron. "We will be down in a moment. Welcome, Cheryl."

"Husband, Cheryl is here."

Seth looked up from his conversation, and a frown creased his brow. Cheryl had learned that while his face often leaned toward fierce, Seth was a good man who hid his kindness under the unconscious glower.

"Welcome, friend." He glanced at Eli. "We were discussing the tragedy that has befallen our friends."

Concern filled Cheryl. "What tragedy? Is there anything I can do?"

Levi gave her a bemused look. "You cannot fix everything that causes suffering, Cheryl."

His words poked her heart in a way she hadn't expected. Maybe she cared too much what he thought and said.

"Have a seat, Cheryl." Naomi placed a platter on the table and then slipped her apron off and hung it on a hook. "And leave our friend alone, Son. You know she has a heart quick to serve and ease burdens."

Cheryl eased on to the wooden bench that lined the large farm table. Levi sat across from her next to Eli and Caleb. His distance opened a chasm between them.

"Many families we know have had their livelihood affected by the Heini's fire. There are other places to sell their milk, but Heini's paid top dollar to keep all Amish milk for their cheese."

"I met a woman today who came into the Swiss Miss to sell some pot holders."

Esther walked in and settled next to Cheryl. "She was so sad."

"Yes." Cheryl nodded. "I asked her if I could buy Christmas presents for her children as a way to help ease their burdens."

"That was very kind, Cheryl." Naomi took a seat at the foot of the table, while Elizabeth sat next to Esther on the bench.

Seth gazed around the room, and then he lowered is head in silent prayer. In unison the others did the same.

Lord, thank You for these friends. Give me peace—she thought of Levi, of Heini's, and of the loss of income for all those families— *peace for so many things.*

Less than a minute later their heads lifted. Naomi passed a bowl of green beans while Seth took a helping of stroganoff and then handed the bowl to Cheryl. "Cheryl, your instincts were good. Providing Christmas presents will ease that family's burdens."

"Could I do the same for other families you know?" she volunteered.

Seth and Naomi exchanged a look, then Seth nodded. "That might help. With assistance from their church districts, the families will be fine, but the extra costs of presents will be difficult to bear."

The conversation moved on from there, and Cheryl let her friend's words wrap around her as she enjoyed Naomi's homemade bread and other delights. As she helped Naomi clean up, her thoughts turned to the Byler families. "Have you heard anything about how Alvin is doing? I was really impacted by what happened at the wedding. To see him being driven away..." A shudder moved down her spine.

"He is fine. Chief Twitchell will figure out what happened, and Alvin will be cleared."

Cheryl wished she could share her friend's certainty.

They worked in silence for a few minutes. Cheryl washed dishes in the large farm sink while Naomi dried them and Esther put them away. Cheryl's phone dinged, and she wiped her hands and then pulled it out. Another text from her mom asking if she had checked the e-Love site brought a groan to her lips.

Naomi paused in her drying to watch Cheryl. "What is wrong?"

"Just another text from my mother. She is intent that I try something that I am not interested in."

"Wait and pray before you respond. Sometimes I have noticed you reply without taking time to think about how you should."

"You're right. I react because I feel like she must have an instant response."

"It is the device. People do not take time to think things through. They all feel they have to respond immediately."

Cheryl nodded. There was something about hearing the quick dings and tones of the phone that had created a Pavlovian response that required instant action. "I will wait to reply tonight."

Maybe if she prayed first, she would find a response that honored her mother's concern while also letting her mother know the site was not for her. Though as Cheryl's gaze drifted to Levi, still sitting at the table talking to his father, she wondered if she'd placed hope where it shouldn't be. Levi had been warm and friendly at first and then became increasingly distant as the night progressed. *If he really cared, then why did everything have to be so hard?*

"What is the source of your conflict with your mother?"

"She is pushing me to try to find a special man, and Momma believes she has the right way to do that." Cheryl's gaze strayed back to Levi, and Naomi touched her arm.

"The right relationship will happen at the right time." Her soft gaze carried concern. "But, ja, it is important not to let seeds of bitterness grow. I am sure your mother only wants what is best for you. Extend grace and the same will meet you from her." Naomi set down the tea towel. "Come. The rest of the dishes will wait. Let us enjoy the fire in the living room."

Cheryl considered arguing, but the remaining dishes were pans that needed to soak a bit. "Sounds wonderful."

The women settled on to the rockers, and the heat from the fire embraced Cheryl in its warm hug. She considered Naomi's words and whispered a quick prayer that God would give her wisdom and peace regarding her mother's current campaign to find Cheryl a man. She had to admit she didn't want to spend the rest of her life alone, but she also didn't want to rush ahead into a relationship when the timing might not be right.

A knock at the door stopped the soft rocking of Naomi's chair. She stood and moved to open the front door. "Lisa, please come in. You are welcome here."

Naomi's small frame came only to Lisa's shoulders. Her dark hair peeked out from under a hat, and Lisa gave the smaller woman a quick hug. Then she slowly unwound her scarf and handed both the hat and her scarf to Naomi.

"Thank you for asking me to come. I needed a break from all the worries about what comes next for Heini's." She sighed as she sank on to the remaining rocking chair. "There is so much cleaning and work to do. But it looks like we can salvage much of the equipment, and only one exterior wall and part of the roof needs to be replaced."

Naomi sat and set her rocker in motion too. The fire crackling was the only sound in the room, other than the occasional squeak of a rocker against the hardwood floor. Cheryl sank into the peace that spread from Naomi to the rest of the room. Her friend's intense sense of calm worked its magic, and Cheryl released the lingering stress of the day even as she wondered what worries and concerns filled Lisa's heart.

The squeak of Lisa's chair stopped, and the woman brushed a strand of hair out of her face, weariness she didn't hide cloaking her face.

Cheryl's heart went out to this woman whom she barely knew. "I am so sorry about all that has happened."

"Me too." Lisa sighed, a sound deep from her soul. "Our family has each other, and we have God, but I hate what our fire is doing to the community. I know it's rippling across the farms. Yet I can't shake the loss of all my grandfather and uncle built. Heini's didn't happen overnight or in one generation. And now in one intentional act, it's all gone."

Cheryl paused her rocking. "Does your father or anyone else in the business have enemies? You mentioned when you delivered the gift basket that he did. Is there someone who would want to destroy the company?"

Lisa started to shake her head but then paused. "I don't like to think that anyone would want to do something so terrible to our family, but someone did." She rubbed a hand back and forth across her forehead. "My father has always trusted people and believed the best about them. Years ago we had an employee, Allen Collins, who embezzled from him. It about broke my father's heart and almost destroyed the business."

"That's terrible." Cheryl couldn't imagine anyone wanting to do something so deliberate and mean, yet it happened all the time.

Naomi studied Lisa with compassion. "Your business bounced back."

"Yes, but my dad and uncle had to start from scratch. That's when Dad started courting the tourist trade. He knew that would be a key to rebuilding the business. To draw tourists to Holmes County, he went to Cleveland, Chicago, really all over the Midwest encouraging people to come to Amish Country in Ohio. He missed a lot of meals at home during that period." Her gaze focused on the fire, but she seemed far away, maybe in the car with her dad visiting all those far-flung cities.

"It must have been a trying time."

Lisa nodded. "But even though Allen embezzled most of the company's money, God blessed Dad. The business flourished—and that spread to other businesses in the area. The crazy thing is that Allen Collins's family remains angry at us. Like somehow our success emphasizes everything he did to steal from Heini's. While we have forgiven him and moved on, they hold a grudge against us." Lisa shook her head. "I will never understand it. Every time we see them in the store, they hurry the other direction."

Cheryl pulled out her phone and entered Allen Collins's name. A grainy photo of him and his wife popped up, and Cheryl froze. Mr. Collins's wife was the same woman who came into the store buying all the Heini's cheese—now she had a name to go with the face: Julie Collins. Cheryl showed the photo to Lisa. "Is this the man?"

"Yes."

Next Cheryl showed the photo to Naomi. "This is the woman who came into the Swiss Miss asking about buying Heini's cheese and saying she wanted to buy all of it she could find." She was also the woman who likely had left the sooty mess for Cheryl and the girls to clean. Could she have been involved in the fire? She would need to mention Julie to Chief Twitchell now that she had a name and picture to give him.

"What about Teddy Harris? Could he have been involved?"

"I told the police about Teddy Harris, but they say he had an alibi," Lisa said.

"That doesn't mean he isn't behind it," Cheryl resumed her rocking. "An alibi is easy to fake." She'd seen that over and over as she'd solved various mysteries and puzzles around Sugarcreek. People often thought they were far more clever than they really were. "The same day of the fire, Julie came into the Swiss Miss, but there was also a young man at Heini's who acted like he was listening to our conversation about the fire. I took a photo of his truck as he left."

"Do you still have the photo?" Lisa paused her rocking, and her eyes focused on Cheryl. She had a look on her face that telegraphed she thought it was important.

Cheryl swiped through photos on her phone until she found the photo and then handed the phone to her.

Lisa studied the image for a long minute, stretching it to enlarge various parts of it before handing it back to Cheryl. "I hoped I'd recognize it, but it looks like dozens of other pickup trucks around this area." She sighed then stood. "But I do think I'll tell Chief Twitchell about Julie. Maybe there's something there. It wouldn't be the first time that family was involved in hurting ours."

CHAPTER FOURTEEN

When Lisa Troyer left to tell the police chief about Julie, Cheryl followed her. Chief Twitchell might not remember her mentioning the fact that a woman had come into the Swiss Miss and been so intent on finding Heini's cheese. If he had followed up with other shop owners, she'd like to know what he'd learned.

The best chance of that happening came if she were with Lisa when the two talked about Julie. It still struck Cheryl as very odd that the woman would make the point of traveling around town to buy all that cheese on the very morning of the fire.

What had the woman been hoping to accomplish?

Stock up on cheese for a decade?

Wipe the memory of Heini's away?

That would be an impossible task for those who had enjoyed the wonderful, artisan cheeses the company made.

She followed Lisa to the police station where Chief Twitchell had agreed to meet them. Could one family hold so much hate toward Heini's? It seemed a long time to hold the backlash of the embezzlement against Lisa's family. Maybe Julie really liked the taste of the cheese and fully understood the importance of the fire before most others did because of her husband's cheese-making experience. That failed to explain away the soot she left behind on the Swiss Miss's rugs, but maybe she had a valid explanation.

Wait, Cheryl. Wait before jumping to too many conclusions. The facts could end up being far different than first impressions indicated.

Cheryl pulled next to Lisa's small sedan in front of the police station, and only one light winked through the large windows in front of the station. As they walked together toward the door, Lisa hummed with nervous energy.

"Do you think he came into the station just to talk to us?"

Cheryl tugged on the front door. "Absolutely. Otherwise he wouldn't have come back in tonight. He could have made you wait until morning, but he knows how this fire has impacted you."

Lisa squared her shoulders and seemed to whisper a prayer. "I hope this information helps him find whoever set the fire."

Cheryl did too. She sat quietly as the large man respectfully listened to her new friend. Although the chief seemed interested, she didn't see any indication that he was ready to race off and question Julie Collins.

"Thank you for bringin' this information to my attention, Lisa. I assure you we are doin' all we can to work with the fire investigator and determine what happened at your factory."

She frowned at the man. "I thought it was clear it was arson."

"True, but there is a lot we don't know. The fire investigator is focused on what was used to start the fire, as well as how it burned. Right now it looks like someone took a few of the wooden pallets you stored the wicker gift baskets on and used that, along with some paper labels, and ignited them. With all the stainless-steel equipment, the fire didn't spread easily."

"We have a state-of-the-art sprinkler system too. I don't understand why that didn't kick in."

"Exactly. The fire investigator is lookin' into all those oddities. My department is helpin' with the theft and also workin' to find the arsonist. I'll talk to Julie in the mornin', but I'm pretty sure we'll find out she's a fan of your cheese." He leaned against his desk and set down his notepad. "You know my wife is a particular fan of your bacon and onion cheese."

"That is a popular one." Lisa sighed, a sound that seemed to stretch up from her toes. "But until we're sure the cultures found at Bylers' are ours, we won't be able to make it exactly the same way. I want to believe the cultures are ours, but what if they aren't? Without the cultures we won't be able to make it exactly the same way."

"So you're thinkin' about rebuilding?" The chief jotted a quick note on the pad then turned his attention back to her. "That's good."

"I don't know for certain. The cultures are a key to the decision. It will be a lot of work between the cleanup and reconstruction, and I'm not sure my father has the heart to rebuild again. We're tackling things day by day. But I hope we will one day be able to relaunch."

After a couple of minutes of small talk, Chief Twitchell ushered the women out of the police station, locking the door behind him.

"Thank you for your time, Chief."

"We'll find the person behind the theft, Mrs. Troyer."

She nodded then turned toward her car. "Thank you for your efforts too, Cheryl. I'll see you later."

Cheryl watched her friend drive away, heart burdened by all that had happened to her. "I wish there was more I could do."

The chief watched her closely, his eyes knowing as he gave a rueful chuckle. "I'd tell you to leave this to the police, but I have a feelin' I'd be wastin' my breath. Remember, I'm used to you pokin' around but the police chief over in Millersburg isn't. He probably won't appreciate you gettin' involved in his case."

Cheryl tried to pretend she was offended by his assessment, but he'd tolerated her poking around the edges of police investigations enough times to know what she'd likely do.

"Promise you'll let me know if you learn anything and leave the real work to me. No one has been hurt yet, and I don't want you to be the first."

"Yes, sir." She always tried to keep him apprised of what she'd learned, even when she got the sense her efforts amused him. At the same time, she'd had the satisfaction of helping people she cared about with the mysteries and problems that plagued them. The cottages nearby that now housed women and children escaping abusive situations were proof of that. She'd never forget the pleasure of when she'd unraveled who owned the coins hidden in mason jars inside the walls of one of the cottages. That money had helped her friend Johnson Williamson finish the cottages that now provided safe havens to these women and their children.

As she drove the few blocks home, many other scenarios like the mystery of the coins filtered through her mind in a collage of images.

After she changed into fleecy pants and a warm top, Cheryl pulled out her laptop and her phone. Finding the photo of the pickup truck on her phone, she expanded the photo until she could clearly make out the letters and numbers on the license plate. She took that number and entered it into Google.

Her Google searches didn't pull up an owner for the vehicle. Apparently, it had been fruitless to think that she could find information like that readily on the Web. Part of her was glad it was so difficult, though the other part wished it had been easy so she could check something off her list.

Then she remembered that Chief Twitchell had mentioned the police were looking for the owner of that truck to ask him about a fire investigation. Maybe if she searched for local news stories related to arson it would help her find information about the young man. In a few seconds she was scanning online articles, trying to identify the stories about recent fires. Several of the articles were dated or not related to the farm fire the chief had mentioned.

She scrolled down another screen of articles and then stopped on one that mentioned names she recognized.

The article detailed a fire that had burned a barn to the foundation at the Myron Mast farm. Toward the end of the piece, Myron's wife, Jessica, was mentioned as having been visiting family with their children. Fortunately the fire hadn't spread, and all of the cattle had been in a field. Still, the loss had been devastating since the barn was filled with equipment for milking the cows. A link to another site told about how the community had gathered around the Masts. Neighbors had even taken their cows to care for and milk until the family could rebuild. Then a month later, there was an article about the barn raising, which included information about neighbors returning the cows.

It sounded like the Masts had a relatively small dairy operation. However, the loss of the barn and equipment would be devastating to any farmer. Then to have the loss of Heini's come so closely on the heels of recovering could only be described as a nightmare. It was little wonder that Mrs. Mast had looked fragile when she'd asked Cheryl to consider purchasing some of her pot holders. The woman was probably desperate for any extra sources of income.

Would providing Christmas for her children be enough?

This poor family might need much more.

And while the other affected families hadn't also lost a barn, it highlighted how precarious their situations could be.

Farming wasn't for those who craved security and certainty.

That didn't stop Myron Mast from insisting in the article that they would rebuild. "This farm has been in my family for three generations. I cannot imagine living anywhere else or doing anything else."

Cheryl's thoughts strayed to Levi. She could hear his smooth voice saying the same thing. Farming and developing their businesses were as much a part of him as his Amish faith.

She entered another search, this one for Allen and Julie Collins. Not much came up. It looked like they were solid members of the community, involved in organizations like their church, a Rotary club, and a couple of community events. She couldn't even find a mention of the embezzlement. Maybe that was old enough it hadn't been pulled on to the Web.

Then she did a search for Teddy Harris. The police said he had an alibi, but that didn't mean she couldn't do a little checking. The Web verified that he was a cheese maker with a plant in Sugarcreek and a large facility that looked an awful lot like Heini's in Millersburg. Maybe imitation was the best kind of flattery, or maybe Harris was trying to confuse purchasers. Either way, it was clear that from the outside, his business was thriving.

There wasn't much that made her think there was an overt feud between the two families. Still, it was good to know more about the man.

She clicked her mouse a couple of times and then typed in the address for e-Love. Mom would ask if she'd spent more time on the site. Had she viewed more than a couple of profiles? Reluctantly, Cheryl pulled up the list of profiles the search engine generated for her. As she scanned the pictures, she couldn't believe she was really on the Web site looking at profiles of men she didn't know.

How could a few words capture who a person really was?

She knew of a few people who had met on similar sites, and those couples did seem happy. In fact, a few of them really had devoted marriages. Even though it was a different way of finding someone didn't mean it was a terrible idea.

As she reached the last photo, though, she couldn't make herself click on it to follow the link to another profile. She might be looking at one picture, but Levi's features seemed superimposed over the image.

She closed the e-Love site and turned back to the notes she'd jotted about the Masts' fire, the Collinses, and Teddy Harris.

Could the Masts' fire be tied to the recent one at Heini's? Had the arsonist used the barn fire as a test to see if he could start a blaze big enough to damage Heini's too?

Maybe there were more ties between the two fires than the Mast farm selling milk to Heini's. She jotted a note to ask Jessica Mast about any other connections that might exist between the two when she took the Christmas presents for the kids to the farm. In fact she'd buy the presents first thing in the morning, then she could deliver them in the afternoon. First she'd call Kinsley and ask her if she was available to work tomorrow. It could be the perfect time to do a little investigating and see if there were any connections between the fires. If there were, it was time to find the arsonist before he or she could start another fire and hurt more people.

CHAPTER FIFTEEN

The morning sky threatened more snow as Cheryl got ready for work. The gray sky was almost bad enough to make her want to crawl back into bed with a good novel and pull a warm blanket over her head. Christmas was two and a half weeks away, and that meant the Swiss Miss would be extra busy. With the help of her team, they'd sell a lot of the unique items she stocked in the shop. In any slow moments, she'd slip out to find the perfect Christmas presents for the Masts' children.

As she did her devotions, she asked God what her gift to Him should be this year. Would He be pleased if she helped more families during the Christmas season? It seemed like such a good thing to do, but was it what He wanted her to do? She didn't want to waste time on the things that seemed good but didn't match His purposes.

She thought about the kids as she drove past the Davies's Christmas tree lot that had been set up at Gleasons' corn maze again this year. A quick look suggested the lot had done a brisk business as people prepared their homes for Christmas.

Beau meowed from his carrier in the passenger seat. She walked most days of the year, but winter weather—and the threatening sky—made the thought of walking home unappealing.

Instead, she pulled into a spot near the Swiss Miss and studied the shop. The large Christmas wreath contrasted nicely with the cornflower blue door. She'd added some twinkle lights to the front windows and window boxes, even lacing them around the edge of the large heart-shaped window. She loved the festive touch those lights added to the store. Maybe this year she'd look for the icicle lights on after-Christmas clearance.

Beau nudged her hand as if wondering what was keeping her in the car.

She shivered. No time like the present to launch into the cold. She cuddled Beau close as she opened the door and shoved out into the brisk wind.

A minute later she'd unlocked the door, and the wind had blown her into the building. Cheryl set Beau down and then flipped on the lights. The room looked welcoming in its soft bath of light even as she shivered. "Time to turn the heat up."

As she walked around the store turning on lights and getting things ready for the day, she thought about the simple routine and how odd it must be for Lisa Troyer and her family not to have a place to do such. It was part of having a store. Not anything she thought about most days. But without those small tasks, she had no business.

In preparation for the Christmas shoppers who would search for the perfect gift, Cheryl borrowed an idea from Heini's and brought out a platter laden with samples of the local cheeses and candy for people to try. She also lit several cranberry and pine candles to help the shop smell like Christmas. Then she filled the coffeepot and the teakettle with water so that shoppers could help themselves to warm drinks, a tasty treat for a frigid day.

Shortly after she flipped the sign to Open, the Swiss Miss filled with the anticipated shoppers. By the time Esther and Kinsley arrived, Cheryl had refilled the cheese sample tray once. The pungent cheese was selling almost as fast as people could sample it. Then Lydia called in with a touch of a stomach bug, and Cheryl knew the day would keep her hopping.

As she rang up another customer who had an assortment of gifts including a slab of horseradish cheese, Cheryl's thoughts again strayed to the fire and the ripple effect the loss had across the community. As soon as there was a lull, she grabbed her coat.

"I need to find some Christmas presents for the Masts' children. I'll be back shortly."

Esther nodded without the usual admonition that she'd be fine without Cheryl. "Kinsley can help me manage for a while. Everyone seems intent on completing their shopping today."

Cheryl nodded. "I'm glad because it's nice to ring up so many sales, but I'm going to need to ask more of our suppliers if they can get me more items to sell. This is a crazy season!"

Kinsley grinned at Cheryl as she walked by with more tea bags and apple cider packets for the drink area. "I'm glad they keep coming because that means you'll need my help for a while."

"Wish me luck." Cheryl grabbed her purse and took a deep breath before heading outside. The wind whisked away her breath before she could take too many steps. Then she walked down the block to By His Grace, where she hoped to find books for each of the children, with her scarf clutched to her face.

When she slipped into that store, Marion Berryhill sat behind the counter, her young daughter resting in the playpen next to her. "Cheryl! I wouldn't expect to see you on one of the busiest shopping days of the year."

"I snuck out for a minute while I can." Cheryl glanced around the Christian bookstore and grinned as she noticed all the people filling its aisles as they looked for gifts. "Looks like you're busy too."

"We like it that way." Marion glanced around the store with a contented smile on her face. "What can I help you with?"

"I'm buying gifts for the Mast children. I'd like to get them each a book, but I haven't shopped for children's books in years."

"Remind me of their ages."

Cheryl rattled them off as Marion led her to a bookshelf in one corner under a hanging cartoon character from a popular DVD series. Once there Marion selected several books featuring Rosie Posie and Meghan Rose. "I love these for the fun characters and the sweet morals. Boys are a little tricky..." But Cheryl's friend still managed to make a couple of suggestions.

A woman waved at Marion from the counter, and Marion shrugged apologetically. "I hope this gives you a starting place."

"It does. Thanks so much."

Ten minutes later, Cheryl walked out with a small bag of books and pencils for the kids. Though she wanted to get something more for each of the children, it was a start.

Before she returned to the Swiss Miss, she made quick stops at Hoffman's Furniture to buy small wooden toys for the boys and at Sugarcreek Sisters Quilt Shoppe for small homemade dolls. If she wrapped each child's gifts in separate gift bags, each would have something special to look forward to Christmas morning. When she showed Esther what she'd selected in one of the rare breaks that afternoon, the young woman agreed that everything would make wonderful gifts for the Amish children.

"You were kind to do this."

Warmth rose up her cheeks, and Cheryl guessed color did too. "It seems small in the face of their challenges."

"It will make a difference for them."

"I hope I can find their farm."

"I will sketch a map for you when we have a break." The bell dinged, and Esther turned toward the door. "I promise."

Cheryl laughed and went back to work. Kinsley had settled right back in as if she'd never taken a break from the store. Cheryl made a mental note to call on the girl if she needed help in the future. Her previous unfamiliarity with the Amish products was replaced with a subtle salesmanship that matched people with appropriate gifts. It was fun to watch her work with the tourists and lead them around the shop.

The shop would need a good cleaning though. The hardwood floors were far from gleaming as people tracked in the light snow. It started in the early afternoon, making a picturesque display in the windows, but it had covered the sidewalks enough to create havoc on her floors. But other than getting the spot mop out every once in a while, there was no point in spending more time on them. As long as people walked into the Swiss Miss, they couldn't help tracking in the snow.

Like Julie Collins couldn't help tracking in the soot if she'd been at the fire.

Cheryl still couldn't think of a good reason that the woman would be there and then in town purchasing all the Heini's cheese she could find. And Julie had been dressed well, not like she'd planned to be at the scene of a fire. Did it matter? Maybe not, but it was odd and out of place. And that made it memorable.

As she followed Esther's map that evening, Cheryl couldn't help thinking of all the other families that had been affected by the fire. Were they getting the help they needed? Was there something more she should do to reach out to them?

Jessica Mast had come into Cheryl's store and crossed her path. They wouldn't all do that. Should she be actively looking for the families, trying to assess which ones needed special help?

Maybe she should wait and see how this attempt went. She'd tried to keep the packages understated, using simple gift bags with plain white tissue paper and little else to add decorative elements.

Cheryl followed the last instruction on the penciled map and turned down a lane that led to a small farmhouse followed by an oversize barn. It seemed like dozens of cows lingered in the pasture despite the winter temperatures. Then she noticed there was a second long barn behind the first. The Masts did not have a small operation with a couple of cows they milked. Had they found somewhere else to sell their milk while Lisa and her family decided what to do with Heini's? Cheryl hoped so because those cows represented a lot of potential milk.

As she pulled to a stop in front of the home, Cheryl noticed a nice foreign model sedan parked in front of the barn. An English man stood in the halo of light filtering from the barn door chatting with an Amish man. She tried to get a closer look at the man, as there was something vaguely familiar about him, but she couldn't figure out why as she squinted to see better through the darkness.

Was he there to negotiate milk prices? That didn't seem too likely, considering his suit.

A window curtain in the home brushed to the side, and Jessica's face appeared in the glass. She smiled and waved to Cheryl.

Cheryl slid from the car then grabbed the box of gift bags from the trunk. She whispered another prayer that she'd selected presents that would please each of the children. She also prayed that none of the children would appear until after she'd transferred the box to Jessica. The purpose wasn't to take the joy of giving from the Masts but rather help them in their need.

Jessica opened the front door as soon as Cheryl climbed the front steps. "Welcome."

"Thanks. If I'd realized you already had a guest, I'd have come another day."

"It is no problem." Jessica paused in closing the door to study the barn. "I did not know he would come on a Saturday." She sighed, a heavy sound that had the echo of heartache.

"Is everything okay?"

Jessica closed the door and turned to Cheryl with a smile pasted on. "Why would it not be so? You have kindly brought gifts for my children. I am so grateful."

Cheryl looked around. "Are the children here?"

"Oh, they are in the barn. Some are doing chores, and the younger ones are helping…although I've heard it isn't much help at all."

Cheryl chuckled and fumbled with the box. "Here, take this. I hope your kids will be pleased. I tried to keep the gifts simple, yet fun and age appropriate."

"I am sure you did wonderfully." Jessica looked around the room. "I will tuck these in the closet away from prying eyes. If you will excuse me a moment."

Cheryl waited in the living room, soaking in the comfortable aura. A handmade coffee table sat in front of two wooden chairs and a store-bought love seat. The chairs had clean lines and the look of quality while the sofa looked serviceable for a house filled with young kids. Colorful rag rugs dotted the floor, one covered with matchbox cars and one with a pillow tossed on it in front of the window. It looked like the perfect place to read a book.

Jessica hurried back into the room, a twinkle in her eyes. "Looks like I managed to hide them. Would you like a mug of coffee? I made some a short while ago." Her gaze drifted back to a window that looked out on to the farmyard.

"I don't want to overstay if you're in the middle of getting supper ready."

"It is on the stove. You must stay for coffee."

"I would like that." Cheryl followed her hostess into the kitchen. While the space wasn't as large as the kitchen at Naomi's, it was lived in. The table was cluttered with books and backpacks, and the sink overflowed with dishes. As Jessica bustled about filling mugs with coffee and placing a few chocolate chip cookies on a plate, Cheryl sank on to one of the chairs at the large kitchen table. "Is there anything I can do to help?"

"No." Jessica set a mug in front of Cheryl. "Would you like cream or sugar?"

"Yes, please." Cheryl doctored her coffee then waited for her hostess to sit. "I was impressed by the number of cows I saw as I drove in."

"My husband has built a nice farm." Jessica played with the rim of her mug. "But we may have to sell. That is why the man is here." She glanced up at Cheryl. "I never thought this would happen to us, but one more disaster, and we may have to move." She shrugged as if trying to dislodge the weight. "The Lord gives and takes away. Myron is convinced this man will buy it all."

"I'm so sorry this happened so soon after the fire."

"Thank you. The community helped us so much. We were able to rebuild better than we had. Now..." Her words trailed off.

"A barn raising isn't enough, is it?"

"Not for this." She swished her coffee. "I don't know how the community can help with this one. We've worked so hard, but we cannot fight everything. Maybe this man is how God will provide for us. The bank loans are too much to repay without the extra money Heini's paid for good, pure Amish milk."

They chatted for a few minutes, but as Cheryl stood to leave, Jessica followed her to the door. "Thank you for letting me come."

"Thank you for the gifts."

"They are small."

"They are the Lord's provision for my *kinder*." Jessica's eyes misted, and she blinked rapidly. "Danki."

Cheryl hugged the woman then hurried to leave before her own tears fell. There was something special about allowing God to use her. It was a feeling she didn't think she'd forget anytime soon.

CHAPTER SIXTEEN

In the twilight, her home felt small and empty. The usually charming cottage set in the heart of Sugarcreek normally felt like a homecoming, but since spending time in homes that bustled with the controlled chaos of active families, the emptiness encased her. She parked in front of the detached garage and then walked through the snow to the back door. It would be months before she'd be able to bring her quiet time back to the patio. With everything covered in a foot of snow, it was almost hard to remember what it looked like in the spring when the new growth started to push out of the soil. And then in the summer when there was so much green and the flowers exploded into a riot of color.

The cold, barren landscape of winter seemed to match her insides. She tried to shake off the mild feeling. This was not who she was usually.

But the loneliness and emptiness of the cottage hit her tonight in a way she couldn't easily shake off. Her days were filled with meaning as she managed the Swiss Miss. And her days were filled with people she cared about and those she could touch for the short time they were in her store.

While Aunt Mitzi had told her to make any changes she wanted to the home, Cheryl hadn't done much. As she unlocked the back door and then entered the kitchen, her gaze fell on her aunt's collection of colorful pottery. So many of her aunt's belongings spoke to her and fit. Why change anything when her aunt had taste similar to hers?

After heating a bowl of chili, Cheryl filled Beau's bowls with food and water before moving to the living room. She built a fire in the fireplace hoping the cheerful flames would warm her thoughts as much as they warmed her body.

Then she sank on to the couch and turned on the TV, but as she flipped through the channels, nothing captured her attention. With the TV a bust, she grabbed her laptop and opened her e-mail. In among the junk folder was an e-mail from her mom. *Why did that end up in junk mail?*

She clicked on the e-mail to open it then slowed to absorb the message.

Dear Cheryl,

I've really been thinking and praying about your relationship with Levi Miller. I know you think this could be lifelong, but I'm not sure you're looking at the situation realistically. I also know these aren't words you want to hear. Maybe that's why I'm taking the easy way and writing them rather than bringing this subject up when we're on the phone.

To you...this is the man you want to share your life with. But to me, I see all the things holding you apart...and the key difference is faith.

Yes, you are both believers, but you can't become Amish. It's not who you are. We wouldn't be able to share e-mails or so many other things. How would you run your business at the Swiss Miss without electricity and the technology you take for granted? But embracing his faith is so much more than abandoning technology. Are you really prepared to do that?

On the other side, he won't leave his faith either. Being Amish is engrained in everything about him. It is integral to who he is and how he sees the world. It wouldn't be fair to ask him to leave his faith. It would change who he is at the core, and that's not love.

Love embraces the person for who they are. Love does not expect them to change to match a mold you have. Yet if you pursue a lifelong relationship with Levi, that is exactly what you are doing. Either you have to change completely or he does. Neither is fair.

I urge you to truly think and pray about your hopes and expectations for your friendship with Levi. Ask God to give you His heart. I love you and don't want to see you hurt. Your hopes are hurting your heart. They're focused on what-never-can-be and as a result you're missing out on what-could-be-possible.

Momma

Cheryl's hands shook as she scrolled back to the top of the message.

Is this what Momma really thought about her friendship with Levi?

Did she really believe that Cheryl was missing out on what could be while she hoped for something more with Levi?

The words stung, and yet there was a ring of truth to them because she'd had the same concerns. Her thoughts had well traveled the path of what-if-I'm-wrong and what-if-I'm-right. She'd considered the possibilities of compromising and becoming Mennonite, but even that would require much sacrifice for both Levi and herself…and was it just too far-fetched? Her head picked up a throb as she read the words again and again. Her mother was a wise woman, but was she right on this?

Cheryl rubbed her temples and read the e-mail again. Then she closed her laptop and stood before heading to the kitchen. She filled the teakettle with water and then set it on the stove. Beau wound around her legs as if picking up on her distress. She picked him up and rubbed under his chin. He purred loudly with a little chirp at the end, then when she stopped, rubbed his head under her chin.

The action made her smile, and she started rubbing his chin again. Tears began to clog her throat as her mother's "focused on what-never-can-be" words echoed through her mind. Was she really crazy to hope that what she and Levi had could become so much more than their current friendship? It sure seemed like Levi was as interested in finding out as she was. And it seemed so wrong to throw that away on the chance that nothing could come from it. The flip side was that something beautiful could come from it, but if her mother was against even pursuing the relationship, what kind of chance did they really have?

Did Naomi and Seth feel the same way? Were they simply too kind to say anything to Cheryl, or were they putting similar pressure on Levi?

When the teakettle began to whistle, she set down Beau and pulled out a peppermint tea bag to put in her favorite mug. After she'd filled the mug with hot water, she carefully carried the mug back to the couch and then sank into the warmth. The aroma began to calm her, but to really reach a peaceful frame of mind she needed to pray.

She bowed her head and imagined she was holding her heart up to God. *Lord, show me the right path. Help me follow You and not what others believe is right for me. I know You know what is perfect for me. I don't want to miss You on something this important, and I don't want to hold back because others are concerned this isn't right for me.*

She waited in that position until her spirit began to settle. There wasn't an audible voice, but there was that gentle calming.

Cheryl blew out a breath then took a sip of her tea.

Lisa Troyer's words about lessons her parents had taught her filtered through Cheryl's mind. Lisa had commented on how her parents had taught her to take risks. *"If you feel it's the right thing to do, you have to take risks. You have to follow your heart."* Lisa had talked about how her parents modeled that for Lisa and her siblings in their business and marriage. *"No matter how hard life got, they always stuck it out. Always."*

Was that what she was supposed to do?

Stick it out through all the doubts and complications to see what could happen with Levi?

If she walked away now, she'd never know if they could have confronted the challenges together. She had a feeling part of her would always feel like she'd walked away before she'd really given them a real chance. That at the first moment people began to say it could be hard, she decided it was too much to risk.

The key was that she and Levi had decided to see what could happen. They hadn't jumped straight into a relationship that was headed to the altar.

No, they were being deliberate and rational. They were allowing their heads to lead the way while their hearts explored whether something more were possible. It seemed like a very deliberate and ordered way to pursue the future. There weren't necessarily the hearts and flowers that romance novels and movies portrayed, but that was okay, wasn't it? She could follow a deliberate path with her eyes wide open—in fact it seemed like her mother had encouraged her to read a book by a marriage expert who urged those seeking a spouse to go into each prospective relationship with their eyes wide open before they shut them once married.

She knew exactly the challenges that stood as obstacles to anything permanent developing between her and Levi, and if she chose to proceed anyway, that was okay. She was doing it knowingly.

That was exactly what her mom needed to know and understand.

Cheryl hadn't been swept away by romantic feelings. No, she had her eyes very wide open. And if she chose to walk the path anyway, then her mother should respect that even if she had misgivings.

She reopened her laptop and e-mail.

Then she paused as she carefully considered how to share her heart with her mom. She whispered another quick prayer then began to type.

Momma,

Thanks for your e-mail. I know it couldn't be easy for you to write, but I appreciate why you did. I also wanted you to know that pursuing this friendship with Levi is something I have carefully considered, and I have and am praying about it.

I think it's really important for you to know that I feel like I need to give everything with Levi a real chance. I don't know what the end result will be. No one can know, but I know I will regret it if I don't let this develop. What if Levi is the one for me and I walk away now? I would always wonder. Finding the right man isn't easy. When I find one who cares for me as much as I care for him, I'd be a fool to walk away. There are obstacles to every relationship, so this one might not develop past friendship, but I'll know that I gave it a chance.

So I've decided not to respond to the requests on the e-Love site right now. I'm not saying that I can see Levi and me together for certain, but he's special enough to me that I won't risk developing another possibility until I know for certain my—our—future. I can't quit on Levi, not yet. I hope you can understand and respect that.

Love you,
Cheryl

Cheryl reread the e-mail then bit her lip as she hit Send. Hopefully, Momma could hear her heart and respect her decision. Maybe the longing for grandchildren could bow to the need of her daughter to find the right man, even if it were in an unlikely match.

Cheryl knew she couldn't quit on Levi...on the possibility of them yet. She wouldn't push things, but she wouldn't walk the other way.

CHAPTER SEVENTEEN

Sunday morning, Cheryl looked forward to looked forward to worshipping at Friendship Mennonite Church until a fresh six inches of snow had her blocked in her home. As she bundled up to shovel her driveway, she wondered if the fire investigator had gotten everything he needed from Heini's. If not, the snow would have done an effective job of covering and probably destroying anything that remained. By the time all the fresh snow melted, in addition to what had lingered from prior snowfalls, anything he hadn't uncovered would be washed away.

As she reached the halfway point in her driveway, a city snowplow turned down her street. Maybe it would clear a path and she could still get to church, but when she reentered her home to warm up, she saw a text that said the service had been cancelled.

She turned on the TV and saw a scrolling line of cancelled services crawling across the bottom of the screen. Looked like the town was going to give the snowplows a chance to do their job before people tried to drive anywhere. Cheryl brewed a cup of coffee and then grabbed an afghan and nestled into the couch, ready to enjoy the peaceful view from her front window.

After she'd warmed up, she read her devotions then settled into a mystery novel. Beau came and curled into her side until he grew bored and left to wander the house, on patrol for something only he knew about.

By the time evening began to fall on Sugarcreek, her street had been cleared and she'd heard many of her neighbors out clearing their driveways and driving down the road. A neighbor with a snowblower had done the sidewalks, a feat Cheryl had watched from the comfort of the couch. If snow fell like this too often, she'd need to invest in one, but most of the snowfalls since she'd moved to town had been a much more manageable couple of inches.

Cheryl was beginning to make supper when her phone rang. When she answered, she was surprised to hear Naomi's voice.

"Please tell me you're bundled up."

"Of course." Naomi's voice had a smile, even though Cheryl imagined she had to be pretty cold. "I did not want to wait to pass this along."

Curiosity filled Cheryl. What was important enough that Naomi would go to the phone shack on a snowy Sunday? "What's up?"

"The snow. About seven inches out here."

Cheryl chuckled. "The wind must be blowing it more where you are."

"It has been brisk at times. But we were able to go to service today." Naomi paused, and her voice dropped. "What I learned bothered me greatly."

Cheryl waited for her friend to continue.

"Several families are exploring selling their farms. More of them relied on Heini's to buy their milk than I realized."

"I know that the Masts are considering a sale. A man was there yesterday to look at the farm."

"They are not the only family. Several more...established families in this area are considering the same." Naomi sighed. "It would be sad to lose so many over this. But what can they do?"

"Aren't there other places to sell their milk while they wait for Heini's to rebuild?"

"Yes, but not at good prices." There was a rustling of fabric, and Cheryl could picture Naomi shrugging in her cape. She grabbed a dish towel and wiped the counters. "Heini's always paid fair prices. Now other places are lowering their purchase price because they know the farmers have fewer options."

"Surely not."

"That is what I heard today."

"Who would have thought the theft of the cheese cultures could cause this?"

"That with the fire has been devastating. Heini's might have recovered from one, but both is too much, some fear."

Cheryl thought about her friends Lisa and LeeAnne as she hung the towel on a hook. They seemed heartier than people gave them credit for, but maybe the cultures were the last straw. "I wish there were something I could do to help."

"It is too big a problem for any of us to solve."

"I'd still like to do something. Will there be a factory raising?"

"Maybe. It all depends on what the Dauwalder family decides. One person says the damage is to one wall. Another says it was to the entire facility. One says the equipment is salvageable. Another says the electrical components in everything were destroyed. One thing everyone agrees on is it is a mess."

"Yes." Cheryl's thoughts wandered to getting Christmas presents for more families, but if they were thinking about selling, the challenges went much deeper than getting presents for the children. That seemed like an ineffective Band-Aid in a dike that was about to explode. Her small effort would be meaningless in the face of the need.

Naomi's teeth chattered, and Cheryl knew she had to get her friend to go home. "Are the roads to your home cleared?"

"They were mostly cleared when we came home this afternoon."

"Then go home and warm up. I will come to you if I can, and we can talk about how we can help these families."

"Be careful." Naomi sounded skeptical. "It is not worth sliding off the road or getting in an accident."

"If I can't get there safely, I'll turn around. But cars have been using my road for the last several hours, so it's worth trying."

She freshened up, and a ripple of hope flowed through her. Together she and Naomi could create a meaningful way to help these families. At least they could try.

Cheryl took her time as she drove through Sugarcreek and found the main roads well plowed. The trucks had done a better job than she'd hoped of pushing the snow to the side of the road, and the Millers must have been out and about even more than going to their Sunday meeting because the road to their farm was pretty clear. If she eased her car down the lane, she shouldn't have trouble keeping it on the path.

A light was on down in the barn, and the warm lights twinkling through the house windows signaled warmth and welcome. Cheryl exited her car, and Esther opened the front door. Cheryl walked through the door and found Naomi sitting in a rocking chair with the fire crackling in front of her. A basket of scraps sat at her feet, and she arranged them in a pattern on her lap for a future quilt.

Cheryl pulled off her mittens and nodded her chin Naomi's direction. "I like those colors."

Naomi looked up at her with a smile. "Tonight is perfect for sitting by the fire and arranging fabric. I may not quilt as much as some, but I enjoy the creative parts of the process."

"I'm always impressed. I don't think there's any way I could put together a pillow let alone an entire quilt."

"It is simple. In fact, come sit next to me."

Cheryl took a seat in the rocker next to Naomi. Her friend was soon lifting the basket and showing her how to pair the different colors to vary the effect. "See how the coral color complements the teal? Then if you add this lavender, it is a nice surprise."

"See, I would have never added the purple."

Naomi shuddered. "Not purple. That would overpower the other colors. But you play with the colors to see what looks best to you. Ultimately that is what matters."

Cheryl began playing with the fabric and soon paired different possibilities. "I can see why you enjoy this." She put a pumpkin-colored square next to a raisin-colored one then made a face. "I don't think I like this one."

Naomi laughed. "It would work with a little help. It could make a nice fall decoration. A pillow or a table runner if there is enough fabric."

"Oh, I don't think so. It's relaxing to play with the colors, but I don't have time to learn to quilt now. Maybe when life slows down."

"I do not see that happening anytime soon." Naomi shook her head with a slight smile curving her lips as she picked up another stack of fabric from the basket. "You have a way of creating adventures."

"I wouldn't mind finding a relaxing hobby or two."

"I believe your way of relaxing is helping others with their problems."

"Maybe." Cheryl hadn't thought that about herself until she moved to Sugarcreek to run the Swiss Miss for Aunt Mitzi. In Columbus, she'd thought she had community. Then she moved here and realized life could hold so much more, and she found herself craving the types of relationships that planted her firmly in the community. If that meant helping people with their challenges, then she would gladly do it. It seemed a natural part of living in community. "I guess I didn't realize what I missed in Columbus. I had my work and a church home, but somehow it's different here."

"You have found your place."

"Maybe it is as simple as that." The use of the word *simple* stood out to her in light of her e-mails with her mom. Would her mom be horrified to know she'd braved the roads to spend time with her Amish friend, when she'd willingly cocooned when church was cancelled due to the storm?

The front door opened and Levi, Eli, and Seth stomped in knocking snow from their work boots.

"Watch the snow." Naomi's scolding held a serious and yet playful tone.

Seth nodded, his gruffness falling away as he watched his wife. "We will take off the boots here and remove them to the kitchen."

"That is better, Husband. Danki."

Seth and Eli didn't bother to slip off their coats before removing their boots and heading into the kitchen. Levi deliberately took off his scarf and then his gloves before raising his gaze to meet Cheryl's. There was no emotion there. The spark that often ignited inside her when she met his gaze flickered and then died. She watched him until he disappeared into the kitchen. She waited for him to look back, waited for...something...but he barely acknowledged her.

His behavior stung. She turned back to the scraps. Naomi reached out and squeezed her hand.

"You must forgive Levi. He has worked hard today to clear the road and keep the animals safe. I am sure he is simply cold and tired."

Cheryl nodded but couldn't speak around the lump in her throat that threatened to choke her. The men tromped back in a few minutes later. Seth settled on the couch while Levi and Eli plopped in front of the fireplace.

"I was surprised to see your car here." Seth eyed her with curiosity. "What caused you to drive here on a day better spent at home?"

"I called her about the families preparing to sell." Naomi glanced at Cheryl with compassion. "I knew she would want to help find a solution."

Seth frowned and leaned forward, elbows on his knees. "Why? It is not her problem to bear."

"It is true." Levi spoke from his spot on one of the throw rugs near the fire. "If the families choose to sell, it is their choice."

Cheryl shook her head. "Without that fire they wouldn't even consider it."

"That we know of." He met her gaze briefly before glancing back at the flames. "Not everyone can share everything that happens easily. Many are more private and keep troubles to themselves."

"Until the decision has been made"—Eli stretched from his place in front of the fire, reminding Cheryl of a self-satisfied tomcat enjoying the warmth—"there is little if anything we can do to change their minds. The decision was not made easily."

"That's exactly why I think we should do something. The fact that the fire is making so many reevaluate what they are doing tells me this is a big problem."

Levi snorted. "Cheryl, you cannot fix everything. This is one that you cannot."

"I saw a man at the Masts'. Maybe he pressured them to sell."

Levi shook his head. "It is not new. Elliott Lawson circuits the farms every winter. It would not feel like the end of the year if he did not visit people, looking for a way to buy land."

Cheryl scowled. She couldn't remember hearing his name mentioned before. "Who is he?"

"A developer. He lives to buy farmland and turn it into something else." Levi shrugged. "If that is what a family chooses, it is their right. You cannot change that decision. But if you really want to do something, there is a benefit planned for the Dauwalder family."

Naomi set the scraps she'd accumulated in her lap into the basket. "The Dauwalders own Heini's."

"Yes."

Naomi turned to Levi. "When did you learn of this benefit?"

"Someone mentioned it at the meeting this afternoon. I was sure you would have heard."

Naomi shook her head. "I had not." Then she shifted to meet Cheryl's confused gaze. "A benefit to help the Dauwalders will also help the rest of the community. The sooner they can reopen, the sooner farm families can sell to them."

"The benefit will be a silent auction of items at the community Christmas dinner. That is really all I know."

"Do you think there will be a community effort to rebuild the factory as well?"

Levi frowned and rubbed the stubble on his cheeks. "I do not know. I asked this morning, but no decision has been made." A large yawn stretched Levi's face. "I will bid you good night. It has been a long day."

"Good night, Levi."

He nodded to her then gave Naomi a brief kiss on the cheek before heading toward the stairs. Cheryl's cheek felt the absence of a kiss, and her heart missed his usually kind words. Naomi caught her watching him leave the room, and Cheryl could almost sense her friend asking her to extend grace to Levi. Maybe it really had been a long, hard day of work for him.

She forced her attention back to the fire. Eli and Seth started a conversation about a project they wanted to try on the farm in the spring, but she quickly tuned it out and shifted closer to Naomi.

"How can I help with the benefit?"

"You could ask Sugarcreek businesses if they will donate items. The more and varied items we have, the more we can raise." Naomi pushed to the edge of the rocker.

"It seems like a lot to ask of people at this time."

"Do not prejudge whether they will be generous. People cannot say yes if we do not ask. Now you should head home before it is too late. I just hope that it hasn't already gotten icy out there."

"You're right, of course. Although it'll be hard to leave this warm fire." Cheryl smiled and collected her things. It would be a long drive home, but she could use the time to plan how to engage the other downtown businesses in these efforts. Sugarcreek citizens had been taking care of each other long before Cheryl had arrived. She'd do all she could to help with that. Her only regret as the miles toward Sugarcreek evaporated was that she still couldn't figure out who was behind the arson. The person was out there, and without knowing his or her motives, it was hard to know if that person would strike again.

CHAPTER EIGHTEEN

Cheryl tossed and turned all night, and sometime in the pre-dawn darkness she'd decided that she'd try to reach Aunt Mitzi when she woke up. It wasn't always easy to reach her aunt by Skype when they'd prearranged a time, but after sending Mitzi a quick e-mail she prayed her aunt would read it and have time to talk. She really needed her aunt's insight and wisdom on the store owners and how best to approach them. It was important to make the right approach so that her requests would be well received, especially in such a busy time of year.

Beau batted at her face in the morning, and Cheryl jolted awake. Her dreams had been filled with shadowy images of children sitting around empty trees as flames consumed first a barn and then a factory.

"Beau, I really want to help them, but it's not easy." She rubbed his ears as he purred. "I really want to find the arsonist. I still can't believe someone would be so cruel as to burn the factory to cover a theft. And to think those cultures are probably ruined, unless they were the ones recovered at the Bylers."

Beau purred, and she sighed. "Sometimes I wish you could talk back, Beau."

But maybe Aunt Mitzi could talk this morning. Her aunt often helped her find angles to the puzzles she worked. If she could do the same with this one, then maybe more than Christmas could be salvaged for these families. Maybe their farms could be saved too.

It bothered Cheryl to think of so many Amish families considering selling their farms. The farms were such an important part of their heritage, and losing them added tragedies upon tragedy.

Before she made her coffee or grabbed breakfast, Cheryl pulled up her e-mail to see if Aunt Mitzi had responded.

Hey, kiddo. I'm here and can wait until nine your time. Skype if you can. TTYS.

Mitzi

Cheryl blew out a relieved breath and wrapped her robe's belt tightly around her waist. She didn't want to take the time to get ready for the day first. Aunt Mitzi would get to see her in her early morning glory—second time in a row. Cheryl sighed but didn't want to waste time on vanity.

She set her laptop on the kitchen counter and opened the Skype program then got a cup of coffee brewing while she waited for Aunt Mitzi to answer. She'd added a bit of creamer and turned the laptop around so she could sit at the kitchen table when Aunt Mitzi answered.

"Thanks for waiting up for me."

"Well, you know I always say sixty is the new forty."

Cheryl laughed. "You do."

"So what has you worked up? Is it still about the Amish families affected by the fire?"

"Yes." Cheryl took a sip from her mug as she collected her thoughts. Then she recounted her conversation with Naomi. "It sounds like several of the families are considering selling their farms. And all of this has come up, as far as we can tell, since the fire at Heini's."

Aunt Mitzi's eyes widened, and she shook her head. "That's terrible. Those farms are so important to the families. Many of them have been passed down for generations."

"That's what I thought." She wished Aunt Mitzi were here and could help her, but the Skype call would have to be enough.

"I really can't think of another time that more than one or two farms have been on sale at the exact same time. It could affect the land prices to have all that land available at once."

"I hadn't thought of that." Cheryl considered that a moment and decided Aunt Mitzi could be right. "The glut of available land could really affect the prices. I wonder who will take advantage of that."

Mitzi's eyes clouded with concern, and she leaned toward the camera. "And whether it's enough to be a motive."

Cheryl nodded. "If someone had a project that needed lots of land, it would be hard to find that readily available."

"And if you could find that much land, prices are so high. The cost could be prohibitive."

"But if you created a situation where people felt they had to sell..."

"Then you could probably get the land at a cheaper price." Mitzi's brow furrowed. "I hate to think anyone would be that devious."

"It doesn't change the fact the cheese cultures were taken before the fire was started." Cheryl chewed her bottom lip as she continued to think. "But maybe that was a smoke screen to make us think the fire was to cover the theft when in reality the theft was a red herring to make everyone think that was the real purpose for the fire."

"Or maybe we're simply overthinking everything." Mitzi pushed back her shoulders and forced a tight smile on to her face. "Maybe it's all a tragic coincidence. Still, I am troubled the farmers are preparing to sell at the same time."

"Do you think they'd look to other Amish farmers to buy the land first?"

"They could, but from what you've described, it's probably too much land to stay in the community." Aunt Mitzi glanced away from the screen and put her chin in her hand like she did when she was thinking hard. "You know, a few years ago I read an article about a proposed housing development that a developer wanted to bring to Sugarcreek Township."

Cheryl frowned. "There's nothing like that around here now."

"I know. The plans got halted when an Amish farmer decided not to sell his land after all. I can't remember who that was though."

"But something like this could cause enough farms to be sold so the development could restart."

"Or the developer could have moved the project to another area. There is a lot of farmland in Ohio that could be turned into a subdivision."

"Thanks for this. I'll get online and see what I can find. Maybe it will be a simple matter to see the development has nothing to do with the fire and need to sell, but if it does..."

"You'll find it. I have faith in you." Aunt Mitzi grinned at her. "I wish I could give you a hug, kiddo. Be careful and don't forget to enjoy the Christmas season."

"Love you too." Cheryl hit the button to end the Skype connection. It wasn't until she hung up that she realized she hadn't asked about the best way to approach business owners. That thought had slipped away when she and her aunt had discussed the Amish farms going up for sale. And the truth was, Cheryl was more excited about Mitzi's information about a failed subdivision development. She immediately opened her favorite Internet browser. It took a couple of tries to get the right search terms, but soon she was scrolling through articles looking for the project Aunt Mitzi had mentioned. There weren't new projects being developed left and right, so she didn't expect it to take long. After eliminating some of the results because of age, she was left with about a dozen articles to skim.

In the sixth article, she landed on the right one. It talked about a proposed development going before the area planning committee for a vote. It sounded like the public reaction to the development was mixed. Some people were concerned that it might affect the character of Sugarcreek by adding a modern, cookie-cutter development on the outskirts of town. Proponents believed it was exactly what the community needed to attract new residents. By providing new housing with the amenities of a subdivision, people who might have been on the fence about moving to Sugarcreek would now commit.

As Cheryl looked around the cottage, she couldn't imagine living in a home without the character that age and love had brought to this home. Yet she'd had friends in Columbus who refused to buy anything older than five or ten years because they were concerned about the maintenance costs. There was definitely a place for both types of homes in most communities.

The next article profiled the development company.

Elliott Lawson was the man communicating with the local government boards to seek approval for the development. Wasn't that the name of the man who Levi said was going around and talking to local farmers? Based on the article, it appeared he was excellent at his job because all resistance from the government had been defused. If he were that persuasive, it made sense that he would also be the one to work with the farmers. The fact the Amish farmers held out when the government caved was impressive.

She did a quick Google search on Elliott Lawson and learned he'd grown up in Germany. He was also the CEO of Lawson Development, a Columbus company that had grown over the years into a regional powerhouse. The company was known for taking pieces of farmland and creating the communities that became the *it* place to live. The developments had more variety than some, so they didn't have quite the cookie-cutter feel of other communities. The photo posted alongside his bio could have been the man she saw in silhouette at the Masts' farm.

As she dug, she found a few online reviews that claimed the houses had shoddy construction, but those were outweighed by many more telling how very pleased they were with their new homes.

Cheryl bookmarked the Web pages and then gasped as she noticed the time. She hurried to get ready and got to the Swiss Miss in record time. As she opened the door for the local residents, Cheryl mulled over what she'd learned. Lawson Development seemed like a good candidate for buying the farmland, but they weren't the only developer in the area. Maybe in the small gap between when the locals took advantage of their hour to get in and out of the Swiss Miss and when the tourists began to shop, she could look into who else had development projects pending with the local planning board.

She smiled as a group of five women came in. It looked like they were members of the Red Hat Society as they proudly wore royal purple and red outfits. One lady wore a dress that combined the two in a clash of exuberance.

"I need something new and different for my kids this year." She looked over red-rimmed glasses at Cheryl with a twinkle in her eye. "A woman can only buy so many soft blankets and collections of hand towels before she knows the kids are prepared for the next thousand years and an ice age."

A couple of her friends elbowed each other and grinned. Another nodded and said, "Ain't that the truth."

"I can help you find unique gifts that will surprise them. How old are your kids?"

It turned out the kids were in their thirties with kids of their own. Cheryl smiled and knew exactly what would break the mold of sameness. Game nights could be a great way to bring busy families back together. She led the women to a small selection of hand-crafted games and Amish-themed games like Dutch Blitz that Lydia had artfully arranged on a table. "These Jacob's Ladders were handmade by men in our community. How about putting together a basket for your kids and their families of games and activities they can do together?"

The women swarmed around the table, and Cheryl was glad she'd had the idea. Maybe she should have Esther put together a few gift baskets of game collections to display. It looked like a hit based on the way the ladies had grabbed baskets and were filling them with items. The one lady with the vibrant dress wandered toward her with a wry smile.

"How many of these games have you played?"

Cheryl glanced in her basket and realized she hadn't really played any of them. "Dutch Blitz...about a year ago...with an Amish family."

The woman chuckled good-naturedly. "When I was growing up, we would gather around the radio and listen to the different shows, a big bowl of popcorn between us and a card game of some sort to play while we listened. With one set of grandparents, I played Canasta. With the other, a great card game called Pitch. You may not have played games recently, but I do believe you've inspired me to find those games and teach them to my grandkids. Maybe we can create some great memories together." The woman's voice wavered a bit, and Cheryl's heart went out to her.

"That sounds like a wonderful idea."

"Well, I have to do something. I have no interest in the video games the kids like to play on the TV."

"I don't know much about those either, although I have played a dance game with some friends. It can be a lot more fun than you expect." Especially when you were willing to look like a fool. She'd been surprised at how much fun she'd had with her friend's preteen kids. She'd danced like she'd never had a lesson, and they'd laughed until their sides hurt. It had been worth every moment of silliness.

The woman patted Cheryl's arm and went back to her friends. "You are a wise young woman."

After filling their baskets with games and toys, the women strolled around the Swiss Miss while Cheryl helped other customers. Esther slipped in with a small wave and set to work ringing up orders before she'd even had time to tie on her apron. It was lunchtime before Cheryl could take a break. Lydia arrived with sandwiches for all of them.

A soft blush colored her cheeks as she handed a small basket to Cheryl. "I thought I would save you the trip out in the snow."

Cheryl thanked her as the aroma of fresh bread tickled her nose and caused her stomach to growl. "I think I'll take this to the office."

Lydia giggled. "I think your stomach agrees. Esther and I can take care of everything."

She closed the office door, and Cheryl sat at the desk, pulling out a thick ham sandwich, a thermos of homemade vegetable barley soup, and a fresh apple. Simple, hearty food that looked wonderful and tasted as good.

It didn't take long for her to inhale the meal, and then Cheryl turned her attention to creating a list of the local businesses to ask for donations for the silent auction. She wished Levi had walked her to her car the prior night and given her a bit more information on how it would work because she didn't know how to explain the exact purpose of the auction. A soft knock pulled her from her list making. "Come in."

Esther slipped inside the room.

"Do you need help up front?"

"Oh no. We have it covered. We have been so busy, I have not had time to give you this." Esther pulled a note-size envelope from one of her apron's heart-shaped pockets. "Maam wanted to make sure you had this. She thought it would help with the donations."

Cheryl accepted the note with a smile of thanks. How like Naomi to be a step or two ahead of her. Esther slipped back into the small hallway, and Cheryl opened the envelope.

Naomi's neat handwriting wandered across the square, neatly listing details about the Dauwalders and their needs. It also contained information about how the silent auction would be handled as part of the Christmas celebration. As Cheryl read about the family's young grandchildren, she decided to make sure they also had Christmas presents under the tree. She thanked God for another family that He'd placed across her path.

She thought about the group of women from earlier that day. A game basket that the whole family could enjoy together might be the perfect solution. She'd consider the perfect items as she worked her way around the downtown businesses.

Cheryl went to the front to check on her helpers. When she slipped behind the counter, the girls had everything well under control. Lydia had taken over at the cash register and was filling a bag with candy that a little boy was carefully selecting while his grandma looked on with an indulgent grin on her face. Esther was helping another customer look at several of the wall quilts. The selection might not have been as large as it was a week earlier, but there were still nice options, and Cheryl knew that Esther would help the woman find the perfect one.

As soon as there was a pause, Cheryl leaned toward Lydia. "I'm going to slip out for a bit. Call me on my cell if you need anything."

The girl nodded, and Cheryl bundled up then headed out the front door. It was time to rally her fellow business owners behind the auction. When the wind slipped down her collar, she shivered, but didn't let it stop her. The thoughts of happy children smiling round the Christmas tree kept her warm as her booted feet carried her forward.

Chapter Nineteen

The sunlight bounced brilliantly off the melting piles of snow as Cheryl left the Swiss Miss. Where a week ago there had been slick sidewalks coated in ice and snow, now small puddles were beginning to form. Even the latest snow hadn't changed that—the sun was out and the snow was giving way.

Cheryl decided to start with the Sugarcreek Sisters Quilt Shoppe. When she entered the storefront next to the Swiss Miss, several people were examining quilts displayed on one wall. In a separate area where bolts of cotton in colorful calico prints lined shelves in a rainbow of color, a couple young women conferred over pink- and raspberry-toned prints. Could they be planning a baby quilt? Muslins lined another wall, and then piles of batting, a wide assortment of threads, and other sewing knickknacks filled shelves and bins close to the cutting table. Agnes Winslow stood at the cutting table, her rusty gray hair escaping from her ponytail as she worked the scissors through a bolt of Christmas fabric.

Cheryl browsed through an assortment of remnants as she waited for Agnes to have a moment to talk. Whenever she came into the Quilt Shoppe, she'd toy with the idea of trying her hand at quilting. But similar to when she'd played with the fabric scraps at Naomi's earlier that week, she'd be overwhelmed in short order with tubs of fabric and no earthly idea how to finish it. So while she enjoyed looking, she knew herself well enough to leave it at that.

Agnes walked to her with a bright smile on her face. "Cheryl, what brings you to the store today? I know the Swiss Miss must be as busy as we are here."

"We are, but Esther and Lydia are handling it. Kinsley is back too. She needs the extra income, and it gives me a little flexibility to work on a couple projects."

"You do like your projects." Agnes listened while Cheryl quickly filled her in on the silent auction to benefit the Dauwalders. "I could donate a gift certificate so the winner could come in and select what they like best. I've found that works better for a shop like mine."

Cheryl watched as Agnes pulled a gift certificate out from a folder behind the counter. "That would be great! Thank you."

After a moment filling it out, she handed the certificate and envelope to Cheryl. "Will this be enough?"

Fifty dollars looked great to Cheryl. She nodded then gathered her courage to ask about the kids. "I feel so badly for these families that are left in financial straits at the holidays. I thought I'd get Christmas presents for the Dauwalder kids. Do you have anything here that might work?"

Agnes glanced around her shop with a frown. "Most of the dolls and few handmade stuffed animals I had are already sold. And unlike city kids, most country kids already know how to sew or learn at home." She shrugged uncomfortably. "I really don't know what to suggest or have anything to donate."

"That's okay. I'm trying to be creative." A flush of heat crawled up her neck at the thought she'd made her friend uncomfortable. "If you had any grand ideas, I was more than willing to pay for them."

Agnes's smile bloomed again as she pushed her glasses up the bridge of her nose. "We'd figure something out, but I'm about sold out. This has been a good Christmas season."

"For us too." Cheryl tucked the gift certificate into her purse. "Thank you for the donation."

"No problem. Try to stay warm."

Before Cheryl left the store, Agnes was back at work answering questions from a middle-aged man looking for the perfect gift for his wife.

Throughout the afternoon, Cheryl checked off visits at various downtown businesses. Ray and Marion Berryhill contributed a cute basket of kid items from By His Grace, perfect for children, especially if they loved singing veggies. Then the Artistic License contributed a beautiful watercolor of a Sugarcreek barn with a buggy in front. Kim Murray contributed a sassy tote bag from her business Buttons 'n Bows. Even August and Greta Yoder had promised to contribute some of their amazing, big-as-dinner-plates homemade cinnamon rolls. Cheryl wouldn't be surprised if their treats had a bidding war.

After dropping off the items she'd collected so far at the Swiss Miss, Cheryl dodged piles of snow and growing puddles toward Hoffman's Furniture. Cars, SUVs, and pickup trucks lined the road until most parking spots were occupied. As she crossed the street, she almost froze. The back of her neck tingled. Was someone watching her progress?

She reached the other side of Main, and she slowly turned, trying to spot anyone who might be watching her. Those walking along the sidewalk looked absorbed in their tasks. No one seemed to loiter or linger near a store in a way that seemed unusual or unnatural.

She shook off her unease and then began walking again.

The feeling grew again as she continued down the block. She took advantage of every storefront window to try to get a glimpse of anyone following her. Still no one looked like they cared what she was doing until she reached Hoffman's Furniture. As she opened the door, she caught a reflection of a young man behind her. He appeared to have stopped to look at some item in the window a couple of shops down the street, but Cheryl couldn't imagine he was overly interested in the items at Buttons 'n Bows. While the store carried an adorable selection of purses, belts, and accessories, it didn't cater to anyone young enough to be his girlfriend.

Cheryl walked into Hoffman's and then waited inside near the door to see what the young man would do. He glanced up, caught her gaze, and froze like a rabbit caught in a flashlight's beam. He abruptly turned and started heading the other way but not before she got a good look at him. She frowned and tilted her head to get a better look. Was that the young man who'd tried to listen to her conversation at Heini's the day of the fire? The one that Chief Twitchell wanted to talk to about another case?

She tried to talk herself out of it. Surely someone wanted by the police in relation to a crime wouldn't hang around downtown Sugarcreek like this young man was. Yet he looked exactly the same.

Cheryl pulled her phone out of her coat pocket and placed a call to the police station. When Chief Twitchell got on the line, she quickly explained whom she was watching.

"I'll send someone over to talk to him. He's been hard to find. If he is who you think, it will be good for us to have a little chat."

Cheryl waited inside the doorway then stepped out of the way as a man entered the furniture store. She sucked in a breath as a police officer walked around the corner. Spotting the officer, the young man took off running. Cheryl craned her neck around to watch, but soon both had disappeared from sight.

"Everything all right, Cheryl?"

Her breath caught again, and she looked back at the man who approached.

Jacob Hoffman looked at her with concern. His tall form with a bit of sawdust around the hem of his otherwise clean jeans looked right at home in the store that was filled with beautiful Amish-made furniture.

She released her breath and then turned away from the street. "It will be." She had done all she could by alerting Chief Twitchell. Now it was time to return to her other task: helping solicit items for the silent auction. But even as she prepared her pitch, questions filled her mind. If that was the same young man, surely he had to be involved, right? But if he was, then who was he connected with?

Finally, why had he been following her? Had he spotted her taking photos of his truck? Did he know she'd gone to the police and that she'd been asking questions around town?

Before she left, Jacob had promised to bring a rocking chair from Hoffman's to the event, then Cheryl continued her loop of Sugarcreek businesses. Molly Bakker added a gift certificate for a two-night stay at the Village Inn Bed-and-Breakfast. Cheryl obtained another gift certificate, this one to the Honey Bee Café, and let out a contented sigh. She'd done a thorough job of collecting nice items for the silent auction. She returned to the Swiss Miss with a light step. Her chest warmed over doing something concrete to help with the silent auction.

Before Esther left the store later that afternoon, Cheryl compiled a master list for the young woman to give her mother. "I'll keep the items I already have on a shelf in the office. Then we'll just need to transport them to the auction."

"Maam will be thrilled to see all these things." Esther glowed with excitement, her red scarf adding to the color blooming in her cheeks. "I will get it to her right away."

"Thanks. I'll see you tomorrow."

Esther paused in the act of tugging her cape tighter around her shoulders. "I will not be here. Remember I asked for the day off so I could do some shopping. Lydia is coming in, and Kinsley will help in the afternoon if you are busy. She promised to check with you at one o'clock."

"That's right. Have a good time. You work so much for me during this season, you deserve an enjoyable break." When Esther had started working for Cheryl two years earlier, it had been a few-hours-a-day job to help in the afternoons. Now Cheryl relied on her so much.

"I will." Delight lightened Esther's brown eyes, and she fairly danced down the aisle and out the door to the street where Caleb waited in one of the family's buggies.

As she worked the last hour before the Swiss Miss closed, Cheryl's thoughts kept returning to Heini's. She hadn't heard anything new about the fire investigation or if the police were any closer to finding the arsonist.

Maybe she'd wander by the police station before she walked home. See if Chief Twitchell had learned anything and if the officer had been able to catch the young man she'd seen downtown. She might be trying her best to help some of the families affected by the fire, but wasn't there more she could do? More than simply calling the police when she noticed something?

The livelihood of Lisa Troyer and her entire family, not to mention so many other local families, was tied to Heini's. The cultures recovered at Bylers were a small number compared to the vast number of cheeses Heini's made. Without those cheese cultures, the factory could rebuild, but it wouldn't be the same and the families might not regain the lost income.

Surely there was something she was missing. And most certainly those answers would come if she just knew the right questions to ask and the right people to talk to.

CHAPTER TWENTY

Delores was collecting her purse and coat when Cheryl pushed through the door of the police department. The basket that had held the birthday goodies still sat on the police receptionist's desk, only now it was filled with office supplies and an assortment of pens.

Delores barely paused as she slipped on her coat. "The chief isn't available right now."

"Do you know how long he'll be?"

"He's talking with some kid they brought in a couple hours ago. I've learned not to guesstimate how long those chats will last."

"I understand."

Delores covered a yawn and then slipped a colorful crocheted hat over her hair. "Is there anything else I can do for you?"

Cheryl tried to think of a legitimate excuse to stay, but it didn't seem fair to ask Delores to stay so she could satisfy her curiosity. "No, that's okay. Can I leave a message for him?"

"Sure." Delores stepped back around her desk and grabbed a sticky note pad. "Jot it on here and I'll stick it on his monitor. He'll be sure to see it that way. The man has a love-hate relationship with his computer. He hates it when it doesn't cooperate, but he loves to stare at it."

Cheryl quickly jotted a note and handed it to Delores. "I appreciate it."

"Sure. I'll walk you out if you give me a minute."

Cheryl glanced around the spare space as she waited for the receptionist to return. A few dated magazines had been tossed on the lone table, and she quickly stacked them before fanning the publications across the desk. Maybe no one would notice, but it looked nicer. Sugarcreek wasn't a place that often dealt with felonies, so most who came in were there to get a question answered, much like she was. Some might even glance through the magazines while they waited. Then she wandered to the bulletin board where community members could post notices. On the board she saw a notice for the Dauwalder benefit and the community Christmas dinner. She'd removed a flyer highlighting a Thanksgiving event when the outside door opened.

Lisa Troyer and LeeAnne Heath stepped into the police station. Faint lines etched the corners of LeeAnne's eyes, and Lisa had dark shadows under hers. Both women gave a faint smile when they saw Cheryl.

"Everything all right?"

Lisa leaned against the edge of Delores's desk and shook her head. "We're not sure."

"Chief Twitchell called and asked us to come in. Well, he asked our dad to, but Dad's not up to being part of the investigation." LeeAnne wiped the corner of her eye and sank on to one of the plastic chairs. "I've never seen him like this, Cheryl."

"He's fought through so many challenges, but this one... He acts like he can't recover from it. It's like all of his dreams were destroyed in the fire. Even though we tell him we can rebuild and it won't take long, he says it's no use. The heart of the company is the cultures. If we could find the rest of the cultures, we could rebuild his dream."

Cheryl stepped closer to the sisters and gave Lisa's shoulders a squeeze before doing the same with LeeAnne. "I wish there was some way I could help."

LeeAnne grimaced. "That's the common feeling right now. I wish I could do something, but without the cultures we're stuck."

"While it looks like the cultures recovered at the Bylers were ours, at this point, even if we found the cultures, I don't expect them to be usable." Lisa rubbed her hands over her face. "Unless the person who stole them knows what he's doing, the rest of the cultures couldn't have survived this long. They're too delicate."

"What about the cultures recovered at the wedding?"

Lisa shook her head. "There were only five cultures, but amazingly they were handled well. But how far will five cultures get us when we used to have seventy? And who knows if we can use them even if they are recovered."

"What my sister means," LeeAnne added, "is that unless it's an expert who has the rest of the cultures we don't expect they'll be viable."

Cheryl remembered what Lisa had told her after the robbery and her research had confirmed. The cultures needed a certain temperature and climate control to ensure they could continue to propagate. The cultures even needed the proper food to continue to live. "I'm still hoping they'll be discovered and still useable," she said. "We can hope, right?"

Lisa grimaced dejectedly. "That would be wonderful but would practically require a miracle at this point. It's been too long since the theft."

LeeAnne touched the silver cross she wore. "I want to believe miracles still happen."

"Ladies, what brings you here?" Delores stopped and looked at the women with lifted eyebrows. "To think I thought I was going home on time tonight." Cheryl almost couldn't make out the mumbled words.

Lisa stepped back and crossed her arms over her chest. "The chief asked us to come in."

"I wish he would have mentioned it to me." Delores sighed. "Let me tell him you're here."

A minute later, Chief Twitchell came into the lobby followed by Delores. "Ladies." He stiffened slightly when his gaze slid to Cheryl. "I guess I shouldn't be surprised you're here too."

"I didn't know you'd called them in."

"Cheryl wants to ask you about the man you're interrogating, Chief." Delores slipped her purse strap back on to her shoulder. "Do you need me for anything else tonight?"

"Just lock the door so no one can come in after you leave. I'll let the ladies out when we're done."

"Thank you. See you in the morning." Delores slipped out the door before he could change his mind.

The moment the lock clicked behind her, he turned his attention to the sisters. "Is it all right with you if Cheryl's here while we talk?"

Lisa and LeeAnne exchanged a look that communicated something only sisters would understand. Then Lisa nodded. "We'd like her to stay."

"Thanks. I promise I'll stay out of the way."

Chief Twitchell scratched his jaw and studied her as if he didn't quite believe her then returned his focus to the sisters. He towered over them in a nonthreatening way. "In the back I have a young man who Cheryl noticed downtown earlier today. One of my officers chased him down, and I've been talking to him since. He claims he doesn't know anything about your fire, but I'm not convinced. I asked you here to see if he's familiar to you. Have you seen him lurkin' around Heini's or Swissters? Do you know him or anything about him?" He paused and studied them a moment. "It's imperative you look at him closely and be sure before you say he might be familiar. It doesn't do any good to pursue him if he's not the right man."

LeeAnne bit down on her lower lip. "Is there any reason to think a young man was involved?"

"Maybe, but I'd rather not explain exactly why. I don't want to color your judgment or memory."

"Okay." LeeAnne glanced at Lisa then back to the chief. "What do you need us to do?"

"We want to cooperate any way we can."

"I'm going to go back and bring him out this way. I've learned about all I can from him, so unless you recognize him, I won't keep him overnight." He turned to Cheryl. "Did you get a good look at him earlier?"

She nodded. "Yes, I saw him. He may have been the young man who eavesdropped at Heini's."

"When we bring him in, I want you to take a look at him. Confirm he is the same man you saw after the fire. Since we know where he lives, I'll have one of my men bring him in."

"All right." Suddenly what he was asking felt grave. If she said the wrong thing, she could cause an innocent man to spend the night in jail. That wasn't something she wanted to be responsible for. Her phone vibrated, and she pulled it out of her pocket. The text was from her mom.

I'VE BEEN THINKING ABOUT WHAT YOU SAID ABOUT LEVI. ARE YOU POSITIVE THIS IS THE COURSE YOU WANT TO TAKE? IT MAY BE IMPOSSIBLE TO OVERCOME THE BARRIERS BETWEEN YOU.

Cheryl wanted to beat her head against a wall. Why couldn't her mom simply accept that this was a relationship important enough to consider and pursue? She hit the button to turn off the screen and dropped the phone into her purse. She'd deal with that later. She'd somehow find a way to help her mom understand that her mind was settled. She didn't want to explore her options on a Web site. There was a living, breathing man in her life for whom she cared a great deal.

Chief Twitchell returned to the back part of the police station, and Cheryl realized she hadn't heard a word he'd said for several minutes, she'd been so trapped in her thoughts.

Lisa pushed away from the desk and started pacing in front of it. "I don't know if I like this. I don't want to identify the wrong person."

"Just look at him. See what you think. That's all the chief is asking."

LeeAnne shifted with a squeak against the chair. "I'll be glad when I can go back to what I do well... running a cheese shop. All of this intrigue and investigating is so stressful."

"It'll be fine." Cheryl wished she believed the words or that she could tell the women she was as nervous as they were. The responsibility settled on her shoulders like a pile of bricks.

The door to the back opened, and Officer Spencer stood to the side so a young man could walk through. In jeans, an untucked flannel shirt, and a heavy ski parka, he looked like he was ready for subzero temperatures. He slouched forward and looked like he'd spent the afternoon worried about every word he said. His cheeks were slack and his eyes dull as he glanced at the women. No flicker of recognition registered, almost as if he were looking past them and trying to forget the afternoon he'd spent at the station.

Chief Twitchell followed him, the chief's gaze bouncing between the women. Lisa studied the man then shook her head with a frown. LeeAnne squinted as if to see him better then did the same. Cheryl took a deep breath as panic began to rise. Could she have been wrong since the sisters didn't recognize the young man? Then she reminded herself police had wanted to talk to him about the Mast fire. It made sense to ask him about Heini's as well. His set jaw indicated he wasn't ready to say anything.

Chapter Twenty-One

An uneasy silence built in the space. The young man finally looked at Chief Twitchell. "Can I leave now, or should I get an attorney?" His words were faintly respectful, but his tone had an edge of belligerence.

Chief Twitchell took one last look at each of the women then hesitated as he looked at Cheryl. LeeAnne touched the base of her neck and then squinted at the man. She turned to Lisa, who looked equally confused. The chief pivoted toward Cheryl and then quirked an eyebrow as if to ask if she thought he was the one.

"Well?" The man examined the chief with an air of impatience as he tapped his foot against the tile.

"Just a minute." The chief never moved his laser-like focus from Cheryl.

Cheryl had no doubt he was the young man at Swissters the day of the fire. "He's the man I saw."

The chief stood a bit taller as he turned to the young man. "You may leave right now, but make sure you stay where I can find you when I have more questions."

Cheryl bit down against a protest because Chief Twitchell phrased it as *when* he had more questions.

The young man sauntered to the door, a bit of a slouch in his walk. "It's been real." He tipped an imaginary cap at them and then unlocked the door and left.

"Thanks for comin' in, ladies."

LeeAnne picked at something on her coat. "I'm sorry we couldn't be more help. I'm pretty sure I've never seen him before. I think."

Lisa frowned and then nodded. "I wanted it to be him, but I don't know." She blew out a breath. "I didn't mean it that way. I really want the right person found so he can get help. We've already chosen to forgive whoever it is for what they've done. It would be nice to know why they stole our cultures, but it really doesn't change anything."

"That's true." LeeAnne brushed the front of her coat and straightened. "Lisa's right, we've given this to the Lord. He has helped us give this up to Him."

Cheryl marveled at the ladies' words, but as she studied the women, she noticed a peace beneath their fatigue and concern. They might not know what was going to happen to their businesses, but it seemed that was okay.

"That's a nice concept, but if we don't find the arsonist, they'll do it again."

LeeAnne patted his arm and then tightened her scarf. "That's your worry, not ours. But I'm as sure as I can be that young man hasn't done anything to make me remember him."

"I haven't seen him around the factory." Lisa hitched her purse back on her shoulder. "If anything comes to me, I'll call."

"Thank you."

The sisters offered small smiles before following the young man on to the sidewalk and disappearing into the darkness. Cheryl shifted and then leaned against Delores's desk. She opened her mouth but shut it as the chief turned toward her. He rubbed his rather long nose then sighed.

"Might as well spit it out, Cheryl."

She pointed toward the sidewalk. "Why did you let him go?" She grimaced as she remembered his cocky, casual strut as he left the station.

"Sometimes you have to reel them in slowly. I'll be watching him closely, but he didn't give me anything this afternoon I could hold him on." The chief ran a hand through his salt-and-pepper hair. "I'll check on him regularly and see what else we can learn."

"I can't say I like it." Cheryl sighed. "He has the attitude of someone who expects to get out of everything. It bothers me."

"Comes by it honestly. His dad is the mayor of one of the neighboring burgs. I've got a call into the law over there, but I also expect a call from his daddy. It seems his father is known for gettin' him out of trouble. I wish his dad could see what his intervention is creating: a young man who doesn't respect the boundaries of the law." He sighed and glanced toward the back rooms. "Is there anything else I can do for you?"

"Have any leads on the fire?"

"You saw my best lead walk out the front door on his own."

Cheryl nodded then decided to take the plunge. "Have you heard that a number of Amish families are preparing to sell their farms? The loss of Heini's as a buyer of milk is causing a significant hardship for many. This might sound crazy, but what if that's the real reason for the fire?"

The chief good-naturedly rolled his eyes. "What do you mean?"

"What if someone got tired of waiting for the land to come available for a development without an incentive?"

"That seems extreme."

"Maybe it is." Cheryl couldn't decide if it were far-fetched or not, but it seemed a viable option. "Aunt Mitzi was telling me about a development that got stalled a few years ago because not enough farmers would sell their land. Maybe that project isn't as dead as it seems."

"Maybe." Chief Twitchell glanced at his watch and straightened even taller than his usual Scarecrow height. "My son has a Christmas band recital tonight, and I promised to be there unless there was an emergency."

"I get the picture." She forced a smile. "I'll head home. Enjoy the music."

"I'll try, if the horns don't squeak and shrill too much." His good-natured smile showed his affection for his son and his activities. "I shouldn't say much since I can't hold a tune on any instrument. See you later, Cheryl."

"Good night, Chief." As Cheryl walked back toward the Swiss Miss, she tugged her collar high against the bite of wind that wanted to snake down her neck. She tried to leave the questions, worries, and concerns behind her and just enjoy the beautiful night. The light poles twinkled with the white Christmas lights, creating an almost magical look for the downtown square. Walking along put her in the Christmas mood. The nativity in front of the evangelical church was backlit and silhouetted by a spotlight. It was hard to believe in two week it would be Christmas and baby Jesus would fill the now-empty manger.

The busy days at the Swiss Miss let her know that it was definitely the Christmas season, but she hadn't taken time to stroll along and look at the lights, absorb the wonders of Christmas, or even decorate much at Aunt Mitzi's. When she thought of the effort of dragging more decorations down from the attic, it seemed like too much work when she was the only one who would see the results. But why was that? Why hadn't she planned some kind of Christmas gathering or cookie exchange at her home? She certainly could if she just planned the details. In fact she'd probably really enjoy the time.

Cheryl turned that over in her mind. Could she pull together some simple time of fellowship that would be a blessing to her friends? Maybe she should try. If it was small, it would at least start a tradition that she could continue and build upon next year.

She stopped to get Beau at the Swiss Miss and then carried him to the car and drove home. But on the way she talked herself out of the idea of a Christmas gathering. It would be a lot of work to add something to everyone's calendars at this busy season, but she could plan now to do it next year.

Beau settled next to her on the couch that night after they'd had their suppers. He snuggled close to her as if he'd been missing her in the craziness of the season. She reached down and scratched around under his collar, and he nudged to her side and purred. All of her Christmas pondering had her missing her family more than usual. They'd always been a close family, but not one without misunderstanding and stress. Her mom's latest decision to pressure Cheryl to find a man other than Levi was a great example. Even so, she loved her mom without question and knew her mom loved her back. She needed to find a way to acknowledge her mom's advice, and even if she chose to ignore it, to show her mom respect.

Sometimes she wished she and her mom could have the easy relationship she shared with Aunt Mitzi, but the dynamic wasn't there. Guess it was the difference between the aunt who could be all fun and games growing up and become a confidante, and the pastor's wife mother who had so many expectations. As an adult, Cheryl could understand the pressures placed on her mother by those in the church, but these same pressures shouldn't extend to her as a thirty-one-year-old with a successful life.

"I want to make her proud, ya know?"

Beau looked up at her with sympathetic eyes.

"You never have mother problems, you lucky boy." She rubbed his ears and then sighed. Deep down her mother wanted the best for her, wanted her to be happy. She may not have the right methods, but Momma's motives were thoughtful. "I need to call Momma and apologize, don't I, Beau?"

He nuzzled a little closer, and she sighed. It was the right thing to do.

She pulled up her mom's number on her phone. "All right, I'll do it."

A moment later she listened to the phone ring and wondered what exactly she'd say. As her mom's voice said hello, she knew she'd have to wing it. Cheryl shot up a quick prayer for help and the right words.

"Hi, Momma."

"Hey, honey. What's up?"

Cheryl inhaled quickly. "Nothing much. I wanted to confirm plans for my trip."

"It will be so nice to have you and Matt and Nicki home for the holidays this year. It will really feel like Christmas to have us all together."

"I'm glad it's working out."

"Me too."

Cheryl gave her mom the flight information, and then silence fell.

"You could have e-mailed that information. I have a feeling this call has more to do with something else. So are you going to tell me what's going on?"

Cheryl sighed and leaned back against the couch cushions. "I wanted to apologize for how I responded when you pushed me to try e-Love."

"Does that mean you're going to try it after all?" The hope in her mom's voice made Cheryl cringe.

"No. I can't, Momma. Much as I'd like to do this to make you happy, it's not right for me."

"You know how I feel about this relationship you think you want with Levi. He's a nice man, Cheryl, but he's not the right one for you."

"You might be right, Momma." Cheryl bit her lower lip, remembering how Levi had acted so distant the last time Cheryl was at the Millers' farm. "But I really need to see this through. Like I said in my e-mail, I'll always wonder what might have happened if I had given us time. Maybe the result would be the same, but I have to see."

"But don't you want children?"

"I do." Cheryl couldn't fight a smile. "But not nearly as much as you want grandchildren right now. I'm willing to trust God for His man and His timing. Isn't that what you raised me to do?"

There was silence, and as Cheryl began to wonder if she'd pushed too hard, her mom inhaled. "You're right. That's exactly what I want for you. And if you think that means waiting to see what happens with Levi, I promise I'll try not to push."

"I like how you snuck *try* in there, Momma."

"I didn't want to make a promise I couldn't keep." The two laughed together, and the tension left Cheryl's shoulders. When they hung up a few minutes later, Cheryl couldn't wait to fly to Seattle. It would be so good to see her parents without this cloud hanging between them.

Cheryl stood and then picked Beau up. "You were right, boy. Talking to Momma was the perfect thing to do."

Chapter Twenty-Two

A couple days later, Cheryl closed the Swiss Miss an hour early so she could attend the community Christmas dinner. She'd already sent Lydia and Esther over with the items she'd collected for the silent auction. After giving the store a quick straightening, she followed her young colleagues to a local church where the meal was being held in the fellowship hall.

The long, narrow space was normally used for youth group functions and the occasional group exercise program. Tonight it was beautiful. A line of artificial pine trees decorated with white lights lined the back wall. In front of the trees, long tables had been loaded with the silent auction items. Next to the last table was an easel with a bulletin board displayed with gift certificates. On the other side, several large pieces of furniture, like the rocking chair from Hoffman's Furniture, waited for the crowd to arrive and start bidding.

As Cheryl strolled the aisle in front of the silent auction tables, she was amazed at the variety of wonderful items volunteers had collected from the businesses in Sugarcreek and Millersburg. There truly was something for everyone.

She watched people start filing through the doors and a lightness filled her chest. It was clear they were there to shop as well as enjoy the community meal.

Half an hour later, the mayor called the buzzing crowd to order. "Well, I can tell you are eager to connect. That's a key part of this dinner, but before we start eating the wonderful food these lovely ladies brought, let's take a moment to pause and thank our Creator for this meal." The moment he finished the prayer he gave directions on which tables won the lottery to go through the food line first. Happy chaos erupted with a scraping of chair legs and cacophony of laughter and discussion.

Cheryl filled her plate with little scoops of a dozen side dishes and one slice of ham. She walked by the dessert table and only selected one cookie. She'd try to fill up on everything else first before getting too carried away with sweets. Mom would have plenty of Christmas treats when she got home—no doubt a plate of her favorite white velvet cutouts and a plate of Matt's favorite thumbprints. Going home was supposed to be like that. The people who loved you and knew you best having the things you love as one way to show they care.

Once she'd picked up a cup of iced tea, Cheryl looked for a table to join. Many of the long tables were already filled with large families. She waved at a few people then noticed a table with the Vogel brothers and Ben's wife. Their contrasting clothes highlighted the decision that had kept them apart for so many years. Rueben wore the traditional Amish clothing with a long, full beard, while Ben and Nelda looked casually dressed. Ben wore dark pants and a long-sleeve, navy button-down, while Nelda had a pair of cream pants and a red cardigan set.

Cheryl approached them with a smile. "Mind if I join you?"

Rueben waved to the open spot beside him. "I have been saving this for a pretty lady, and you fit the bill even if your hair is so short."

"Rueben." Nelda breathed the word with her eyebrows arching into her feathered, gray hair.

"It's all right. I like his sweet talk." Cheryl grinned at him before setting down her plate and taking the seat next to him. "Why haven't I seen you fellows in the Swiss Miss more this week?"

Ben elbowed his wife. "Nelda's decided to keep me busy with all kinds of errands. You'd think after so many years of marriage, I'd be used to all the extra activity around Christmas."

"You should have stayed with the simple life then." Rueben's words did not bring the conflict they once would have. Instead, Ben good-naturedly rolled his eyes.

"You've forgotten all the extra work Maam had us do, not to mention all the extra work your good wife went to. Bless her heart, she could bake like the whole town was going to stop by her door for a treat."

"That she could." Rueben got a distant look in his eyes. "I do miss her angel food cake. That woman could whip the eggs like no one else."

Conversation interspersed with enjoying the good food filled Cheryl with a sweet warmth. She loved this town and the people like the Vogels who filled it. Then the Berryhills joined them with their little girl. The young toddler was dressed like a princess but wailed like a little waif who hadn't had a long enough nap. Stress etched lines around Marion's eyes. "Do you mind if we join you?

We're running out of spots, and Eden's fussiness is not making friends." She blew a piece of hair out of her eyes. "It's been one of those days."

Nelda reached for the girl. "Let me hold her while you eat."

"Be careful, she might get food on your lovely sweater."

"No worries. Clothes can be washed, but little ones can only be loved on for a season before they grow and leave the nest. Isn't that so, sweetheart?"

When things had settled down and Ray and Marion had eaten a few bites from their plates, Ben started the conversation again. "Did any of you hear that the Lawson company is ready to relaunch its plan for that subdivision?"

Rueben froze with his fork halfway to his mouth and then snorted. "That always struck me as a fool idea. Who would think that Sugarcreek needs a subdivision? Look at all the houses that are for sale in town. Seems there are enough for anyone who needs one."

Ray wiped his mouth with a napkin. "Didn't the original plan fall apart because of the land?"

Ben nodded. "The company couldn't get enough farmers to sell land to them. Seemed they had grandiose plans and expended a lot of money before they had the land lined up."

"Cart before the horse," Rueben muttered. "Fools."

Cheryl put down her silverware and placed her elbows on the table before propping her chin on her hands. "Why do you think the plans have resurrected?"

"Someone is selling them land."

Eden squealed, and Ray handed her a piece of roll.

"But it must have been the same land that they tried to develop before, right?" Cheryl asked. "Seems that land would have to be located in a certain place. The approval the company received was for a specific location. Wouldn't they have to go back to the planning commission to get approval for a new site?"

Ben nodded. "I've heard they have to get a development up and going or they'll run out of funding. Banks aren't willing to loan them more money without a project to back it. Let's get the mayor over here. He'll know about the permit." Ben waved a hand in the air until he caught Mayor Clayton Weller's attention. He gave the lady he was chatting with a quick smile then headed toward them.

"Are you enjoying our community dinner? The ladies worked hard on the food."

"It's wonderful." Cheryl held up a red velvet cookie. "These are amazing."

"My wife loves to make those." Clayton patted his trim belly. "I'm glad she brought dozens of them here. It makes it less likely I'll eat all of them."

"I remember when my wife would do the same." Rueben's gaze took on a distant look again for a moment. Then he seemed to bring himself back to the moment. "But we called you over for an important question."

The mayor looped his thumbs in his belt loops. "Sure. I'm happy to answer anything I can."

"Is that Lawson company back to work on its development?"

"I've heard rumors, but hadn't heard anything concrete. Its project was before my tenure."

Rueben nodded then pointed at Ray. "This man had a good point, one I wanted to hear your take on. If the company buys different land from the one it got approval to build on, would the company get to build or have to go back for approval?"

Clayton rubbed his chin as he considered the question. "I think we'd want the plan to be reevaluated to make sure it was still in the best interests of Sugarcreek. I don't want anything to happen that would affect the nature of our fair town. Tourists expect a certain look, and I don't think subdivision developments fit that."

"If we agree with you, should we lodge a complaint?" Ben leaned forward, and then Nelda patted his hand. "I want to make sure the right process is followed if we want to make sure everything is on the up-and-up."

"Sure. I'd contact the board. Or give my office a call tomorrow and I can explore further."

"I think I will do that." Rueben and Ben shared that nonverbal communication that had developed between them. "Thank you for your time, Mayor."

"Sure thing." He glanced around the table with the fixed smile of a politician. "Enjoy the rest of your evening."

Cheryl watched him move to the next table and strike up a conversation with Jason MacLean and his family. She was a little surprised to see them at the community dinner since their new farm-to-table restaurant, the Chicken Pluck, was still getting firmly established. Still, it was great to see them making the effort to be part of the community.

Rueben rapped the table with one hand. "I think I shall stop by the mayor's office Monday after our checkers game, Ben. See if I cannot get him to dig into the development."

"Sounds like a solid course of action." Ben nodded toward the silent auction tables. "Should we do some shopping, Nelda?"

She leaned toward Cheryl with a pixie look on her face. "Did I hear what I think I did? Did my dear husband give me permission to shop?"

"He did, and I know for a fact all of the proceeds are going to a needy family."

"My favorite kind of shopping." She smiled at her husband with a twinkle. "I think we should Christmas shop. I have my eye on the rocking chair. It would look great on our porch."

"Let's go see it." He stood and then helped Nelda from her chair. "Enjoyed sharing the meal with you."

After they moved toward the tables, Seth Miller moved to stand before the microphone near the small stage. He eyed the microphone as if it were a foreign invention that might sting him. He stood in front of it a minute, then Levi slipped up next to him, turned the microphone over, clicked a switch, then tapped it and handed it back to his father. Seth accepted the mic with a grimace and then turned toward the tables. "Thank you all for joining us for the community Christmas dinner. Many thanks to all the women who provided the wonderful food."

A rolling round of applause filled the large space. Cheryl swiveled in her chair to find Naomi, but her friend must have been hiding. Cheryl made a mental note to tell Naomi how wonderful everything was when she did see her friend.

The microphone hissed, and Seth held it away from him as if afraid of what it would do next. Levi eased it back toward his mouth, and then Seth lowered it again before continuing. "As part of our gathering tonight, we are hosting a silent auction to benefit the Dauwalder family. Many of you know them, and those who might not, know their cheese. The Dauwalder family runs Heini's, and a fire heavily damaged their factory a week ago. While the police work to find who set the fire, we want to help them with rebuilding efforts. A world without Heini's special cheese would not be right. So before the carol sing-along, please take a few minutes to shop in the silent auction. We will close bids in half an hour. Also, if you would like to join us for an old-fashioned factory raising, the Amish community plans to tackle that project next week if the weather cooperates. With one main wall to rebuild and a portion of the roof to repair, it should be a doable project. Contact myself or my son Levi. Danki."

Seth handed the microphone to his son and then hurried toward the kitchen as if afraid he'd be asked to use the technology again.

Mayor Weller closed the auction forty minutes later and then invited the Baptist choir to the small stage to lead the group in several Christmas carols. While "Joy to the World" filled the room, Cheryl walked back to the silent auction tables to see how she could help. In short order, she had her phone out and was running tallies of those who had placed the winning bids on various items while others helped group the items by winner. As the song changed to "It Came upon a Midnight Clear," the women made a master list of how much each winner owed. Then Cheryl added a credit card reader to her phone so people would have another way to pay.

"You do not need to do that." Naomi's voice was soft but firm.

"I want to. And this will help make sure that the Dauwalders get everything. I'd hate for someone to not be able to pay because the husband didn't know how much the wife had bid and they didn't have sufficient cash or a check with them."

"What about the fees?"

"I will donate that. Call it my contribution to the Dauwalders' cause." As Naomi started to protest, Cheryl held up her hand. "It won't be that much, and it's my pleasure. Let me do this."

"All right." Naomi nodded, and her kapp strings bobbed next to her chin. "Danki."

An hour later Cheryl helped the other volunteers reconcile the amounts people had paid with the amounts that were owed. "Everything balances. Great job, everyone."

When she reached Aunt Mitzi's cottage, she opened the front door with a soft sigh. It had been a long day, but a good one.

Beau wound around her feet and meowed at her like he hadn't seen her in days and was dying of starvation and neglect. She picked the Siamese up and tickled under his chin. "It hasn't been that long, boy. And I know for a fact you had a full food bowl when I left. I am certain you won't die of starvation anytime soon."

He followed her as she hung up her coat and set her purse on a side table. She walked through to the kitchen and turned on the stove. Hot tea seemed like a wonderful idea.

As soon as the teakettle whistled, she filled her favorite mug with the hot water and then slipped a peppermint tea bag into the water. She settled at the small kitchen table and picked up the week's edition of the *Budget*, the Amish weekly published in Sugarcreek. One of the lead articles was about the fire at Heini's. Beau leaped onto the table and walked across the paper before settling in a circle on the right-hand side of the spread.

"Beau, what are you doing?"

The cat looked up at her with doleful eyes but didn't move. She nudged him with her hand, but he started grooming a front paw like he didn't have a care in the world. Well, he didn't since she catered to his every whim. Surely he could do her the favor of getting off the paper so she could finish reading the article.

"Come on, Beau. Get up, boy."

He kept grooming.

"Fine. You have to get off." She gave him a harder nudge, and he stood with a huff. Then he stretched each of his front legs, then his back legs, before settling right back where he had been and started to wash his face.

"All right, mister. You leave me no choice." Cheryl scooped him up and set him on the floor. Then she looked at the paper and froze.

The article Beau had covered was all about the new development. A sidebar mentioned that the company hadn't developed a new project in two years and needed a fresh one for the infusion of capital that would come. Next to the article was a photo of Lawson shaking hands with Myron Mast. A cunning smile lit up Lawson's face as he grinned into the camera. What was the man up to?

As she studied his picture, Cheryl knew it wasn't anything good.

She examined Myron's sad countenance and knew it wasn't for the good of that family either. How many more families would the man hurt in the name of helping a poor Amish farmer out before he had his development purchased?

CHAPTER TWENTY-THREE

S nowflakes floated leisurely through the air as Cheryl scrambled from her car to the Swiss Miss's front door. The weather forecast called for flurries throughout the day, but the last time that had happened, Sugarcreek received four inches and it was a long walk home. Today Cheryl wasn't taking any chances on repeating that cold walk. She'd even left Beau at home since he'd seemed less than thrilled at the prospect of climbing into his crate. He'd flat out refused.

Cheryl smiled as she walked past the heart-shaped window that remained her favorite feature of the Swiss Miss. That one window seemed to symbolize everything that Aunt Mitzi had tried to create: a store where showing God's love mattered as much as selling a dozen of the most beautiful quilted pot holders and Amish dolls. Cheryl had tried hard to convey that same approach as she'd taken on the responsibility for the store.

As she passed, Cheryl brushed snow off the ledge of one of the empty flower boxes. Today that was probably futile, but she didn't want to let the pile get too deep. Once at the small alcove in front of the door, Cheryl tugged her keys from her coat pocket. She was sticking them in the lock and starting to turn the doorknob when she noticed an envelope taped to the corner of the door.

What on earth?

She finished unlocking the door then grabbed the envelope and carefully tore it from the door, frowning when she saw the smear of tape goo left behind. That wouldn't be easy to remove in these cold temperatures.

She fumbled with the envelope, breaking the seal as she entered the Swiss Miss. The store was cool, but still warmer than the outside. She hurried to turn off the security alarm and adjusted the thermostat so the customers wouldn't freeze. Then she took the envelope and everything else to the long wooden counter at the back of the store. When she slipped the card from inside, she saw that it was plain, buff-colored paper.

A typed message was on the paper.

I know who stole the cultures. I'll meet you behind your shop at noon. Don't tell the police or I won't come. I will know if you call them.

Cheryl reread the message.

Why wouldn't they want the police involved? Because they had something to hide or they were afraid of someone who did.

Cheryl studied the card and prayed about what she should do. If the person was willing to come to the shop, then she wasn't in any real danger. She could simply let whoever was working know she was stepping out for five minutes, and that if she didn't come back in that time, they should come check on her. It couldn't take longer than that to find out whatever the person knew, and then she'd know whether the information was worth giving to the police.

With Christmas so soon, Cheryl really couldn't afford to be too distracted from the Swiss Miss. Esther and Lydia were doing an amazing job keeping everything running, but the truth was it was her store and she owed it to Aunt Mitzi to make sure she did a great job. After all, the profits from the store helped support her missionary work in Papua New Guinea. While the Swiss Miss did fine, the Christmas season was critical to the overall profitability of the shop. All the time she'd taken to help with the Dauwalder and other projects was time she couldn't invest in the shop. Aunt Mitzi deserved her best efforts—though it was her aunt who had encouraged her to get involved.

Cheryl shook her head and had to laugh at herself. She could overthink anything.

God, help me to do the best I can with each task set before me. I know You can help me get everything done that I need to today. Give me Your wisdom and Your grace.

Peace pushed out the worries as the prayer slipped through her mind. What a great reminder that God knew her best and knew how best to help her manage her time and her endeavors.

Twenty minutes later she set the envelope on the desk in the office and then gave the floor a quick sweeping. She straightened a couple of the displays on the round tables that dotted the store's floor and then restocked a couple of areas. By the time the Vogel brothers knocked on her door, she was surprised to see that she was late.

"I'm so sorry."

"No problem, Cheryl." Ben winked at her as he shook snow off his coat and then stepped inside. "We were having fun watching you work until the snow got a little cold."

Rueben shook his head, his beard scattering snowflakes as he did. "He is soft. That is all there is to it. I told him to go with me to the Honey Bee Café, but he refused. He liked watching you better for some reason."

"Well, I'm honored, but I'm glad you knocked. Let me get the coffee going while you set up your game."

The soft sounds of the brothers playing checkers filtered to her as Cheryl kept up her efforts to clean the store. She needed to see if she could get more items from a couple of her Amish vendors. The soy candles and homemade jams had been selling like crazy the last few days. It was always a challenge to try to predict what items people would focus on in each season. In each week even! She only had two of Jessica Mast's pot holders left. Maybe Esther could get a message to her to see if the woman had any more of them she was willing to sell.

The door opened, and Lydia and Esther walked in, full of giggles and with rosy red cheeks. Cheryl looked beyond them to see Levi climbing back into the buggy.

"I'll be back, girls."

Esther gave her a knowing look before heading to the office to hang up her cape.

Cheryl ignored the girl and headed out the door. "Levi?"

He turned to her, and his lips creased in a welcoming smile. "Cheryl. Is it not too cold to be out here without a coat?"

"I'll be a minute, but I wondered if you would be in town through lunch."

His eyes were warm and seemed to look deep into her, the way they used to. "I can be if you need me."

Warmth climbed her neck, and she wished her skin wasn't so fair that every flush of heat was visible. Maybe Levi would interpret it as something to do with the cold. The first tourist bus arrived, and Cheryl stepped to the side to allow the first guests to pass by her. She cleared her throat and forced her thoughts from his warm gaze. "I found a letter waiting on the front door when I got here. The writer claims to know who took the cheese cultures and states he or she will meet me behind the Swiss Miss at lunchtime."

"Is not this something you should tell Chief Twitchell rather than me?"

"If the person hadn't told me not to contact the police."

"I do not like the idea of you meeting with them."

"What else can I do?"

"Ignore the letter." His words were punctuated with a frown, and he hunched his shoulders.

"Levi, I can't. I have to meet with whoever this is and see what they know. What if this is the difference between finding who stole the cultures and set the fire and letting them get away?"

"Do you really believe that you are the only one that can do this? Let the police do their job. Chief Twitchell is good at what he does."

"Yes, but the letter specifically said no police." Cheryl bit down the sharp words she wanted to say. Why was Levi being so difficult? Didn't he understand that she had to do this? The letter didn't give her any options...

He blew out a breath and straightened on the buggy seat. "Since I cannot change your mind, what do you need from me?"

To know what our future holds. To know that you care even half as much for me as I care for you...

The words trailed unbidden through her thoughts.

Where had that come from? Cheryl shoved her hands in her pockets as her fingers began to go numb. Her heart also felt numb, as if it were drifting away from Levi. When had he stopped being a safe haven?

She blew out a breath and watched it freeze in front of her as she tried to frame her thoughts. She needed him to smile at her and wrap her in a warm hug, but since she couldn't expect that—

"Cheryl?" The word was abrupt and sharp, and it pulled her from her spinning thoughts.

"Would you come back and wait with me for this person? I need to know you are here." *For me.* "I'm not sure who the note writer is and would feel better if you are here."

He looked off at the horizon as if examining his calendar and then nodded. "I can. I will return at noon."

"Thank you."

He tipped the brim of his hat and then flicked the reins to urge the horse forward. Cheryl watched him merge the buggy into traffic before turning back to the store. The conversation had been harder than she would have expected. There was some barrier between them that she couldn't identify. Some barrier they had to scale. Had somehow stating that they both wanted to see where their relationship could go put a pressure on Levi that he didn't want?

The questions ricocheted around her mind as she reentered the Swiss Miss. While she'd been talking with Levi, the Annie's Amish Tours bus had pulled up down the street. Many of those tourists had gone straight to the Swiss Miss and were now happily shopping and filling the baskets Lydia had handed out. Cheryl pasted on a smile as she headed to the back table to make sure the coffeepot and hot water carafe were both full. Then she refilled the tea bag basket. Before she finished, several of the tourists had followed her to the table and were happily chatting about the remaining people for whom they needed to purchase gifts.

Cheryl tried to focus on their words. Her mind worked hard to select items to show them, but she couldn't pull her thoughts together. Not when her mind was so jumbled wondering what would happen at noon and what Levi thought about their friendship. Her whole life felt inside out, and she was ready for something to settle into place. Ready for some answers.

CHAPTER TWENTY-FOUR

Right at noon, Levi appeared in front of the shop. He waved at Cheryl then wandered around the store before reappearing a few minutes later. Cheryl brushed her sweaty hands down the front of her apron and then started to untie it as he stopped in front of her.

"I am here as you asked."

"Thank you."

"I did not see anyone when I walked behind the store. Do you want me to come with you?"

"I don't want to scare away whoever is waiting. Do you mind waiting behind the door? Then if I need you, I can knock and know you will be right there."

He studied her intently. What did he see? "If that is what you want."

It didn't matter what she wanted. She had to find out whether the person was coming and what they knew. "I think it would be best. Thank you for being here."

He nodded then followed her down the hall to the back door. "Should you get your coat first?"

"I don't want to take any longer than needed. This gives me a good excuse to get back inside."

She froze at the door, and Levi reached out and squeezed her hand. "You will be fine. I am a knock away."

"Yes, you are." She blew out a breath and then squared her shoulders and pushed out the door. When she reached the back area, no one was there. She checked her watch. She was here exactly when the letter writer had asked. She hadn't talked to the police. So where was he?

About the time she was ready to go back inside because the cold had penetrated her sweater, a young man stepped around the corner of the building.

"You." She breathed the word as she recognized him. It was the same young man who had been listening in to that first conversation between her and Naomi back at Heini's. The one who had followed her and then she'd seen at the police station.

He held out his arms. "It is me."

"Who are you?"

"You don't need to know my name. But many consider me the much maligned."

"Usually if the police want to talk to you, there is something prompting that."

"Maybe, but not this time."

"Yet you want to tell me something you know about a crime, right? Why don't you just tell it to the police?" She crossed her arms and pulled them in tighter, hoping to hold in some of her heat.

"Let's say I trust you more than I trust them. Haven't you seen all the headlines about police violence?"

"But none of those places are anywhere near here—and Chief Twitchell wouldn't allow anything like that to happen in Sugarcreek."

"Maybe, but I need to know if you're going to help me or not."

"Help you how?"

The young man sighed and dropped back against the Swiss Miss's wall. His shoulders slumped, and he looked dejected. "I didn't mean to cause so many problems."

"Oh?"

"A man hired me to burn the Masts' barn. I needed money—a thousand dollars is a lot—but now I wish I'd never met him."

"Who hired you?"

"I'm not sure I should tell you."

She stamped her feet on the ground and moved from side to side, trying to warm up. "Then why tell me any of this? Are you wasting my time? Because frankly it's cold out here, and I have other things to do if you aren't going to tell me the truth."

He sighed and looked pained.

"Why don't we start with the easy information? What's your name?" His answer would let her know if he was finally willing to cooperate.

He groaned. "I don't want to go to jail." He squared his shoulders and looked at Cheryl. "Billy McCullar." The words were so quiet that Cheryl wasn't sure she'd heard them correctly.

"What?"

"Billy McCullar. My name is Billy McCullar, and I burned the Masts' barn so I could have some money to get out of Ohio. With my dad as mayor near here, I live my life under a microscope. Everyone has a say in what I think and do. I'm sick of it."

"I don't know, but most teenagers feel like they're living under a microscope, especially living in a close-knit community. It doesn't mean they burn down buildings."

"The man told me that if I did, he'd pay me a thousand dollars. I guess I got caught up in how much money that was." He shoved his hands deep in his coat pockets and then looked up at her with regret shining in his eyes. "I didn't think about how I'd feel to see the Masts all over town and know that I had caused their loss."

"How did you do it?"

"Gasoline and a match. The barn planks were old, lumber dried out, and the fire took off before I expected it to." He looked down and kicked at a loose pebble. "I didn't know what I was doing."

"Okay. Did you burn down Heini's?"

"No." The word burst from his lips. He pulled his hands from his pockets and held them in front of him. "The man asked me to, but I refused. I didn't like how I couldn't shake the first fire from my mind. I wasn't going to be part of a second."

"So the same man hired someone to start both fires."

"He tried. I don't know for sure who set the second, but since he asked me to do it..."

"Yes, it seems reasonable." Cheryl fought back a shiver. She couldn't stand out here much longer, no matter how repentant he was. "Why are you telling me all of this?"

"I want you to investigate. The police will stop looking once I confess to the Masts' fire. That's enough to make them believe I did both, but I didn't. I'm willing to accept the consequences for what I did, but not for someone else's crime."

While that made sense, she still wasn't sure why the young man would pick her to confide in. "I need more than that. Who hired you and asked you to start the second fire?"

Billy looked away from her, a shadow falling over his face. He swallowed convulsively several times, and she could see the fear in his eyes.

She offered what she hoped was an understanding look. "I want to help you because I want to help the Masts and Dauwalders. But that means I need more information." As it was, Chief Twitchell probably wasn't going to be happy with her. He tolerated her looking into mysteries and puzzles so long as it didn't interfere with his investigations. This was getting dangerously close to doing exactly that, since both were active cases.

"I don't know the man's name."

She stared at him. He'd agreed to start a fire and commit a crime for someone he couldn't identify?

He must have read the skepticism on her face. "Really. I tried to track him down after he asked me to do the second fire, but he cleaned out his account. It was gone."

"His account where?"

"Facebook. Obviously using a fake name. That's how he contacted me. I got a message with information, and he sent more details when I agreed."

"How did he know you would do it rather than contact the police?"

The man shuddered. "He said he'd hire someone to kill me."

The words settled like a lead weight over them. The door opened, and Cheryl jumped as Levi stuck his head outside. "Everything okay?"

"Yes." She tried to block his view of Billy, but she couldn't hide her shiver. Levi nodded and closed the door, but a minute later he reappeared with her coat.

"It looks like you need this."

Her heart warmed at the thoughtful gesture so reminiscent of the man she had fallen in love with. "Thank you."

He nodded then pointed back inside. "I'll be there like we discussed if you need anything." He waited for her acknowledging nod and smile before shutting the door again.

"You—you told someone? You told that man, didn't you?"

"I told my...my friend...that I was talking to someone. He didn't see you. He's not one to pry like that. I promise."

Cheryl used the time it took to slip into her coat to organize her thoughts and questions. "So the man contacted you via Facebook, but when you started to have questions, he'd closed his account."

"Yeah. That's exactly what happened."

"Okay, that will make things harder, but do you have the messages?"

He shook his head. "I didn't think to print them off until they were gone. I was so stupid."

She wanted to agree. Who could think burning down a family's barn was a good way to earn money? Maybe there was a clue in the way Billy was paid. "You said he paid you a thousand dollars?"

"Yes."

"How did he get the money to you?"

"He sent me a message via Facebook to look for the money in a trash can downtown."

"In Sugarcreek?"

"Yes, downtown Sugarcreek."

Downtown had a lot of traffic, especially this time of year. The man would have had to leave the money in the middle of the night and trust that it would be there when Billy went to collect it.

"He told me to get it by eight o'clock or he wouldn't guarantee it was still there." He looked each way and then back at Cheryl. "I was pretty dumb, wasn't I?"

"Yes. When are you going to talk to Chief Twitchell about the Masts' barn?"

The man gulped, and his face paled. "Tomorrow. After the factory raising. I want to make sure I can help with that."

"Okay. I will ask him Saturday if he's heard from you." Billy needed the accountability. It would be so much easier to get into his beater pickup truck and keep driving.

"I will do it." There was a force to his words that made her believe him.

"Good."

"You'll look into the factory fire. I didn't do that one."

"I'll try." She didn't want to give him false hope. "It'll be hard without more information, but I'll try."

"Thank you." Even though he'd admitted to a terrible thing, he seemed less burdened as he walked away from the Swiss Miss.

She hoped he understood how serious the consequences could be. She watched him turn the corner. There was no sugarcoating it. This young man was going to learn some hard lessons in the future. She hoped they made him a better man on the other side of the experience.

CHAPTER TWENTY-FIVE

As he promised, Levi waited inside the door when Cheryl reentered the Swiss Miss.

"Well?"

She shook her head and held up a hand. "I need a minute to process what he told me."

Levi waited patiently for a minute then asked, "Did he start the fires?"

"Not at Heini's. He thinks he knows who ordered that fire, but has no real way to identify him." She leaned against the wall next to Levi. "It's so sad, Levi. He's thrown away his life, yet he's so young. I don't think he understands what it means."

"If he was involved in the Mast fire, they may forgive him and not get the law involved."

She had seen such grace extended, but did it really help the person who committed the crime to either feel like they'd been punished for what they did or to avoid feeling like they got off scot-free? Still, she had seen this Amish way of extending grace and forgiveness work amazing healing in difficult situations. She couldn't help feeling sad to think of the pain and hardship that fire had caused.

"Who has something to gain from the Masts' and Heini's fires?"

She didn't realize she had spoken out loud until Levi's focused gaze rested on her.

"It is a good question."

"Billy's comments make it clear he believes the same man ordered both fires. If that's true, then there had to be a reason. The challenge is identifying it. Maybe once we know that, we can figure out who the person is."

Levi nodded. "I will think on this as I work today." He pushed off the wall, but then turned to Cheryl. "Will I see you tomorrow at the factory raising?"

"I think so. I'm going to have Kinsley work most of the day. That way Esther and Lydia can help in shifts as well."

"There will be little for the young women to do. There are not as many families that will make an event of the raising. It is too cold."

"You're right. I'll bring drinks out as soon as I know the Swiss Miss will be fully staffed. With Christmas getting closer, I need to make sure everything is ready for the tourists before I leave."

"All right. I will look for you." He hesitated, and his hand started to come up as if he wanted to brush her cheek. She willed him to do it. She longed for a simple touch from him, yet he turned and walked out the back door.

Cheryl wilted against the wall, wishing she could demolish whatever was standing between them, but until he told her what it was, it was hopeless. *Lord, I need help to understand.*

While she might long to stay there and try to figure out what was wrong with Levi, there was too much to do. As she and Levi had stood there, she'd heard the bell over the front door announce several customers. She owed it to the girls to get out front and help. As she did, her thoughts kept turning over what Billy McCullar had told her. Someone had hired him to burn the Masts' barn and tried to hire him to torch Heini's. He hadn't done that, but someone had.

Who could profit from both locations burning?

She thought about where the Mast farm stood in relationship to Heini's. They weren't close enough that causing one to close and the other to sell would be enough land for the development.

In a spare moment, she slipped into the office and called Mayor Weller's office. Maybe he could tell her if Lawson Development had done anything about updating permissions for the development. If it had, then there'd be a record of where the subdivision would go. At least there should be.

"Mayor Weller speaking," he said as he answered the phone. His voice sounded more formal than when he was out at the community event.

"Hi, Mayor. This is Cheryl Cooper. I wondered if you've had a chance to check into the subdivision."

"I've got a call into the planning commission. Shana said she hadn't seen anything new, but she'd check with Lawson Development to see if there was anything they needed to do before proceeding."

"Okay. Would you mind letting me know what you learn?"

"Happy to." He paused a moment. "None of us want the character of Sugarcreek to change. You can be sure we'll keep a close eye on this."

"Thanks." Cheryl hung up, glad to know the mayor was doing something about their previous conversation, but also concerned that the company might hide its plan if it was indeed trying to resurrect the subdivision. Was there any way that she could dig up that information faster than the mayor? If she called the planning commission, she'd be replicating Mayor Weller's efforts. But maybe she could call the company.

Cheryl stepped back on to the Swiss Miss's sales floor long enough to make sure the girls were still managing everything well. Then she picked up the White Pages. Not finding Lawson Development in there, she opened Google and did a quick search. A minute later she dialed the number and waited for someone to answer.

"Lawson Development."

"Hi. I wondered if I could talk to someone about your Sugarcreek development."

"Sugarcreek development?" The woman sounded confused. "I'm not sure what you mean."

Cheryl took a second to think up her cover story. It would have been smarter to do that before she called, but she could come up with something.

"Hello?"

"Sorry, a friend had told me that your company had plans to build a subdivision near Sugarcreek."

There was a clicking noise as if the woman shook her head and her earring jangled against the phone. "Not that I know of. I'm not privy to all plans, but if there was something major going on, I'd be told about it."

"I saw Mr. Lawson at a farm near Sugarcreek. Doesn't that mean you're working on a project?"

"Not necessarily. Mr. Lawson receives many requests for appraisals and offers to sell. If he's intrigued, he checks those out personally." She chuckled, a warm, soothing sound. "He always says that if he wants to know if a project has real potential, he has to see the land himself. Photos aren't enough for him."

"He sounds very dedicated."

"Oh, he is. It's one reason the company's been so successful. If you give me your name and number, I'll be happy to call you after I check on your question with Mr. Lawson."

"Thank you." Cheryl decided to leave her information and then hung up. If the receptionist didn't know about a Sugarcreek project, it wasn't definitive proof that it didn't exist, but it sure did lean that way.

She pulled up the company's Web site again. Would a legitimate company like that risk hiring someone to set fires?

It didn't seem like Lawson Development would need to if the information on its Web site was accurate. It looked like a midsize company that worked throughout Ohio with an emphasis on the area from Columbus north to Cleveland. Sugarcreek fit in the middle of that area, so it made sense that the company would want to expand into the area.

Well-functioning companies didn't often cross the line between legal and criminal activities. She hopped over to the Ohio Secretary of State's Web site and did an entity search for Lawson

Development. The information that popped up didn't tell her if the company was on sound footing, but it did tell her that it actually existed and was in good standing.

She stared at the computer screen. What other questions could she ask?

The mayor was working on it from the government side, and she'd left a message with the company.

That seemed about all she could do without another clue to follow.

Someone rapped on the office door, and Cheryl looked up to see Lydia standing there. Strands of her long black hair had escaped from her bun and threatened to tangle with her kapp strings. More customers must have come in because Lydia looked frazzled.

"What can I help you with, Lydia?"

"There is someone here who insists on seeing you. I told him you were busy, but he is most insistent."

"No problem, I'll be right there."

Lydia disappeared, and then Cheryl ran her fingers through her short hair. She hadn't looked in a mirror for hours so hoped she didn't look equally as frazzled from all her searching. She pulled a tube of tinted lip gloss from her desk drawer and swiped it across her lips before standing and heading to the front.

When she reached the front, a man about her age leaned against the wooden counter. He appeared to be examining the candy in the various bins, but she wasn't so sure he cared about sweets. Lydia pointed toward him, and Cheryl squared her shoulders before heading his direction. She pasted on a bright smile and stopped next to him.

"Can I help you?"

The man looked up, and his grin practically blinded her. His teeth were so white. "You're even prettier than your picture."

Her picture? She studied the man and knew she'd never seen him before. "I'm sorry?"

"When I saw your profile on e-Love, I decided I wouldn't wait for you to accept my request to communicate. The only thing that would do was to get in my car and come meet you. Lucky for me you were here, at work."

"I usually am." She tried to maintain her smile. She'd looked over the e-Love site and nowhere did it say where she worked. "I have to confess I'm a little confused. How did you say you found out where I worked?"

His grin wavered a bit, but his eyes were sincere as he pulled out his phone and with a few clicks turned it around so she could see a photo of herself. "Your profile is new, and I have family who lives here. I know it's a small place. I just asked the checker at the grocery store if she knew you. She recognized you right away."

His grin widened. "I've been on for about six months, and yours was the first profile that captured my imagination."

She didn't know whether to be flattered or terrified. Who would hop in their car based on a photo? "Where did you say you were from?"

"I haven't yet." He held out his hand. "John Chancey from Columbus."

She shook his hand and tried to cover her confusion. "It's great to meet you, John, but I'm afraid this has been a huge mistake. You see, I'm not the one who set up that profile in the first place."

"Well, I should thank whoever did. Someone hasn't already jumped in and claimed you, have they?"

"Oh no. You're the first." Cheryl resisted a shudder that wanted to course through her. What a mess. "And coming all this way...I'll have to tell my mother the trouble she's caused you."

Understanding began to dawn in his eyes. "The Mom Syndrome."

Cheryl tilted her head and studied him.

"The one where Mom decides you're not moving fast enough or she doesn't like the man in your life, so she takes a few steps to give you options."

"I didn't know that was a thing."

"Moms do it to their sons too. Ask me how I know."

They shared a smile, and Cheryl handed his phone back. "I won't know for sure until I call her, but the Mom Syndrome fits." Boy would her mom get an earful if this hypothesis was correct.

"So you're not looking?"

Cheryl shook her head.

The tall man stuck his hands in his pockets, and a bit of color crept up his neck. "Well, I always say if you want to score big, you've got to swing for the fences. Sometimes you hit the ball, and other times you move air." He tipped an imaginary hat toward her. "Thanks for your time. I hope you have a great Christmas."

"Thank you." She watched as he turned to leave. "John?"

He paused and looked back at her.

"Thank you for the compliment."

It was his turn to look confused.

"It's not every day that someone drives a couple hours to come meet me."

He nodded and then walked out of the store.

Lydia approached her with a wary glance. "Everything okay?"

"It will be after I talk to my mom."

She could figure out who had ordered both fires later. First she had to call her mom.

CHAPTER TWENTY-SIX

When Cheryl got home, she was still miffed at her mom. She should have been bolder and just told her mother what she thought about the profile from the beginning. She should have just turned it off.

She shot her mom a quick text. CALL ME AS SOON AS YOU CAN. THANKS.

Her phone rang twenty minutes later with a call from her mom as she sat down to eat. "Hi, Momma."

"What's up, Cheryl?"

"I had an interesting visitor today."

"Oh, someone I know?"

"I don't think so, but he saw my profile on e-Love and hopped in his car to come meet me."

Silence. That was all she got from her mom.

"I know you meant well, but Sugarcreek isn't a big place like Seattle. It's easy to track people down. What if he had been a stalker or wanted to do something to harm me?" Cheryl blew out a breath and told herself not to erupt. "I should have thought of this. I should have just taken down the profile when I first saw that you set it up."

"Who's heard of a man seeing a photo and hopping in his car?"

"It happens, Momma. It happened to me today. It was awkward. You should have asked me before setting up a profile on a dating site."

"At least I picked an adorable photo."

Cheryl clamped down on her bottom lip to bite back words she wanted to say. "A photo of me in Christmas pajamas. Really, Momma?"

"You're right, and I'm sorry." Her mom sighed, a weary, sad sound. "I shouldn't have pushed so hard, and I hope you will forgive me."

"I . . . I do." Cheryl sank on to one of the kitchen chairs. "Please trust me in this, Momma. I want to find a man to share my life with, but it won't be through a Web site like that. At least not right now. And I don't have time to deal with this..."

"All right, I'll take everything down tomorrow."

"Tonight." Cheryl grimaced. "I don't want any more unexpected visitors."

"You're right, dear. I don't know what I was thinking." Her mom laughed, and then they chatted a few minutes about Christmas plans. When they hung up, Cheryl felt like progress had been made.

The next morning Cheryl packed a bag with work clothes in case there was anything she could do to help when she got to the factory raising. She wore a pair of navy pants with a festive Christmas sweater, not exactly clothes to do manual labor in. She knew she'd get to the Heini's location and want to do more than watch. It wasn't in her nature to sit passively by while everyone else did the work.

As soon as Lydia and Esther arrived and Cheryl confirmed Kinsley was still coming in, Cheryl got in her car. She stopped at the market for a couple cases of water then drove to Heini's. The parking lot was overwhelmed with buggies and pickup trucks. Despite Levi's assurance that it would be a family affair, it looked like half of the community's able-bodied men had shown up with the intent to build.

As she stepped from the car, she tugged her coat collar closed. The sound of hammers and power tools echoed across the open space. A group of about twenty men cleared away the last of the debris from what remained of the factory wall that had collapsed while another group cut framing pieces of wood to size for the project. The pile of wood being cut to size stood next to an even bigger stack of plywood. A final group of men was beginning to lay out the pieces for quick use once the foundation in this area was cleared. Fortunately, the foundation hadn't been damaged in the fire, so the group only needed to rebuild the wall and a portion of the roof.

When she thought back to how destroyed everything had looked right after the fire, it felt like a miracle that only one wall had sustained heavy damage. However, the fire had successfully distracted everyone from the fact that someone had stolen the cheese cultures.

Maybe it was a good thing Billy had said no to committing this arson. He'd burned the Masts' barn down completely. Because this fire hadn't been as thorough, Heini's could reopen in a few weeks if all went well.

And if that were the case, did the Amish farmers really need to sell?

The thought bounced around her mind, and she realized if they could hold out for a few months, Heini's would start purchasing the milk again. Then the farmers would regain this key source of income.

Someone jostled into her, and Cheryl jolted from her thoughts.

Cheryl searched for Levi in the crowd. He, Seth, and Eli would be in the thick of the activity, and she had no doubt they would be some of the very last to leave.

As she surveyed all the activity, rebuilding looked doable in a day or two. There would still be immense amounts of cleaning and inside work before Heini's was ready to begin making more cheese, but getting this wall up was a key part of the process. When her gaze searched the group working on cutting the wood to size, it collided with Levi's dark blue eyes. A small smile lit his face before he turned toward a man who extended another two-by-four to him.

The men had an effective system, and Cheryl loved watching the methodical way they attacked the challenge. She had little doubt they would have the wall up by the end of the day. The roof wouldn't take long either. Then the Dauwalders could focus on cleaning and sanitizing everything before creating new cheeses based on new cultures.

As she watched the work, Cheryl knew they could rebuild and be a stronger business on the other side of this challenge. It was more than possible. With support like this from the community, such an outcome was almost guaranteed.

Wouldn't other communities be stronger if they could band together like this?

So many problems could be solved if people would set aside their differences, real and perceived, and focus on helping each other. She loved that aspect of Sugarcreek. Her life had changed when she accepted Aunt Mitzi's invitation to come manage the Swiss Miss, and she was so grateful to understand what it meant for communities to take care of their own in meaningful ways.

Cheryl headed toward a few women who gathered near a tent. The tent was large enough to host a wedding reception, and it provided a small bit of shelter from the cold. Inside were several long tables and folding chairs. One table had been set to the side and was sagging beneath trays and pans of food. Next to it were several coolers filled with water and Gatorade. "I have some water in my car if you need it."

Almina Troyer, Lydia's mom, stepped forward and gave Cheryl a warm hug. "I believe we have plenty, but danki for thinking to bring some."

Cheryl returned the hug and then stepped back with a rueful smile. "It looks like you have plenty of everything."

A woman swept into the tent, arms laden with baskets of dessert items. "You just think it was overflowing before." The twinkle in her voice alerted Cheryl that it was Naomi before the woman set down the baskets and then tugged her hood off. "It was goot of you to come."

"Do you need any help?"

Naomi's eyes sparkled as she looked from woman to woman. All shook their heads. "We are fine." Naomi stepped closer. "Are you here to see a specific young man?"

Heat crawled up Cheryl's neck, and she turned away from Naomi. "Of course not. I'm here to help if I can."

Naomi gave her a side hug and then tugged her toward a table. "We can sit here until the men need us."

"Shouldn't we do something?"

"Not if there is nothing to do in the moment."

As Cheryl sank on to a chair next to Naomi, she pondered her friend's words. They could form a new Amish proverb, so much truth resided in the words.

Naomi reached over and patted Cheryl's hand. "Do not overthink everything. There is a time to be and a time to do. This is the time to rest before the next burst of activity. More activity always comes."

"That's true."

"Of course." Naomi leaned closer, and a small frown wrinkled the corners of her eyes. "What has happened between you and Levi?"

"I don't know." Cheryl sighed and then met Naomi's concerned gaze. "He has started to distance himself. Maybe he's changed his mind about me. About us."

"I do not think so. Maybe he is taking time to pray for guidance. That would be a good step."

"Yes, it would." If only she could believe that was really what had him staying away from her when a simple smile would mean so much to her.

A woman waltzed in, clad in designer jeans and a fluffy coat with fur-trimmed hood that looked like it belonged on a ski slope. When she knocked her hood back, Cheryl bit back her surprise.

"Julie Collins?"

"Yes, she and Allen have been here since the beginning this morning. She only left to get more donuts. Claims more were needed." Naomi rolled her eyes, and Cheryl bit back a smile as Naomi pointed to the large platter already waiting on the table. "That woman has not learned the value of sitting still."

Julie waved to the ladies. "Where would you like this box?"

Almina hurried to the table. "How about you place them under the platter and then the box will be ready the moment we need the extra donuts."

"Perfect." Julie set them down with a flourish then frowned. "Have you seen Lisa or LeeAnne?"

Naomi pushed back from the table. "Not yet. They will come when they are ready."

"Sure, sure. I wanted to see if they need anything." Her shoulders slumped, and then she sank on to a chair at another table. "I feel so bad for them." Then she brightened. "With all these men, the building will be ready to reopen in no time."

"After sanitizing everything." Almina looked through the tent's opening at the construction. "That will be a large task."

"Sure, but it's a doable task. It is better than not having a factory at all." She looked at Cheryl and quirked her head to the side. "Have we met?"

"You came into my shop. The Swiss Miss."

"Oh, that's right. I was desperate to buy all the Heini's cheese I could as a way to support the Dauwalders. I knew they'd need the income if any of it was on consignment."

"Do you plan to eat it all?"

Julie waved a hand as if batting a fly. "I couldn't, though I wouldn't mind trying. Some of it I'll freeze for later, lots I'll give away to friends. Watch out, Sugarcreek, you're getting cheese for every celebration."

"It's a good thing I love the cheese then." Cheryl smiled at Julie's enthusiasm.

"It seemed like the only tangible thing I could do to help them." Julie chuckled uncomfortably and shifted in the chair. "I know how silly it sounds, but I needed to do something. You should see my fridge though. It is overwhelmed with cheese!"

Those didn't sound like the words of a woman who had tried to destroy the company.

"Oh, what's happening out there?" Julie leaped to her feet and hurried out of the tent. Cheryl followed her, curious to see what had caused the sudden burst of movement.

Lisa Troyer, LeeAnne Heath, and their parents stood near the men cutting the wood to size. They appeared to be thanking the men for their help and paused for a longer time with one man. Based on the photos Cheryl had seen online and the way Julie was hurrying toward him, the man was Allen Collins. When she reached the cluster, Cheryl overheard Allen's words.

"I'm so sorry for the pain I caused your family in the past. I hope you will forgive me."

Mr. Dauwalder nodded regally, but a genuine smile lit up his face. "Of course, Allen. It happened years ago and worked to our benefit in ways I could not have imagined at the time."

Lisa slipped her arm through her dad's. "God often does that."

LeeAnne nodded. "What is intended for evil often works for the good of His children."

Allen glanced around the damage with a grimace. "I'm not sure how this fire does."

"If nothing else, it gave you an opportunity to be freed from your past guilt." Mr. Dauwalder stood even straighter. "That is a gift that I will accept as good." He glanced at the activity buzzing around them. "This too will be rebuilt. We will reopen. And we can make more cheese."

Lisa looked at her father with admiration in her eyes. "I am so glad to hear you say that, Father. I was so worried you would decide it was time to retire."

"Notice I said *we* would do all those things, Daughter. It must be a family effort."

"It will be." LeeAnne's voice throbbed with promise, and she leaned over to hug her dad. "It would have felt wrong for Heini's to disappear. It all sounded and looked so bad right after the fire, but this is something we can do."

Allen stepped forward and took Mr. Dauwalder's hand. "If there is something I can do to help, please let me. It would be a privilege to work with you again."

Mr. Dauwalder nodded. "I appreciate your offer." He turned to his girls. "We still have many friends to thank for their help."

The three walked toward the cleanup efforts, and Cheryl felt a new lightness in her chest. The fire had brought reconciliation to a broken relationship. Truly a miracle in the light of a terrible event. *How like God.*

Now if they could only find the lost cultures or know once and for all if they were destroyed.

Chapter Twenty-Seven

The men kept working, the sound of their activity creating a background harmony of hammer strikes, saw buzzes, and ringing of the dumpster. Cheryl chatted with the other ladies a bit before she grabbed one of the coolers of water. "I'll take the water to them. The men are working too hard to stop."

Naomi and Almina smiled at each other. "That sounds like our men." Naomi nudged Cheryl. "Make sure you take a special bottle over to the saws. There is a certain young man who would like one from you."

Cheryl shook her head as the other ladies chuckled. "Naomi, you are incorrigible."

"No, just interested in your future." The woman grabbed a bottle of water. "But if you are too busy, I will be happy to take one to him."

"Oh, I have it." Cheryl slipped from the tent to the music of laughter. If one sign of good friends was the way they could tease you mercilessly, then she had some exceptional friends.

She started with the men who were about done with the cleanup. "Looks like you could use some water."

Jacob Hoffman shook his head. "It's so cold out here, it's hard to tell if we've worked up a sweat."

"All I have to do is look at that pile of trash to know you've done a great job." Cheryl made sure each man got a bottle, chatting with them the whole time. Then she moved to those who were starting to place the skeleton of two-by-fours for the new wall. Her steps began to slow as she overheard one of the men talking to another about the Teddy Harris cheese factory.

"If you are still looking for a job, the Harris plant is hiring." The man didn't stop working as he talked.

"I just need something to fill the gap while I wait for Heini's to reopen. Might feel odd working for the competition."

"I hear you, but bills do not wait."

The second man harrumphed. "That is truth. What positions are they hiring?"

"All types. Sounds like their business is booming as restaurant and grocery stores scramble to fill the orders Heini's had. Christmas is a big enough season."

"True." The man wiped a coat-covered arm across his forehead. "Maybe I will apply. I need the income."

"Kids need food."

"And clothes. Jonathan has decided to jump two sizes. My wife is beside herself finding ways to make his old pants work."

"Kids do that. Tell her to stop feeding him Miracle Grow." The two laughed as they continued working.

Cheryl's thoughts ran through the information. Teddy Harris was hiring. Sounded like the company was taking full advantage of the hole Heini's closing had created. It could simply be a smart business decision or it could be part of a long-term plan to overtake

Heini's. Was it really possible that another business would act that way here? Sugarcreek wasn't exactly New York City.

But with all the information she'd learned as she looked into people like the Collinses and others, Teddy Harris seemed to be the one with the most to gain from Heini's going out of business. No one else was expanding their business as a result of the Dauwalder's misfortune.

Even with the resurrection of the building that was happening all around her, the Dauwalders would struggle to recreate what they'd had without the cultures. And Teddy Harris would know exactly how to use the cultures and protect them while he had them. Few others would understand the extremely delicate nature of the cultures. And the police had only found a few of the cultures at Alvin Byler's home. The rest were still out there somewhere. Those five would give Heini's a start. It might not be the full array of seventy varieties they'd made before, but it was a start.

When she approached those at the saws, Cheryl saw that Alvin Byler had joined Levi. The man didn't attempt to run the board across the saw, he left that to Levi, but he hauled two-by-four after two-by-four to Levi to be cut. Cheryl waited to the side until the men noticed her and Levi turned off the saw.

"Cheryl." Alvin nodded toward her. "Danki for your help the day of the wedding."

"I wish I could have done more." She set the cooler down and flexed her fingers and wrists.

"It is all right." Alvin shifted his feet but didn't leave. "The police decided I could not have started the fire. They finally believed my wife and family that I was at our home working on my wife's to-do list for the wedding. That woman had a list a quarter mile long."

Levi grabbed another board. "Women tend to go crazy preparing for events like that."

"They just want everything to be perfect." Cheryl tried to keep her frustration with Levi from coloring her voice. "I'm glad to hear they aren't focused on you anymore."

"Me too." Alvin shuddered. "I never want to experience something like that again. What bothers me is that I cannot determine who would have slipped those in my fridge."

"There were so many people at your home that day."

"Yes, and they were all friends. It pains me to think one of them would have done something like that and then told the police to come."

Levi set the wood against the saw and then pulled his gaze to Cheryl's. "Sometimes people are not as they seem."

"Yes, sometimes. But others are everything they seem. Most people are that way." Would Levi understand? Why did he act as though he thought she was the one who had changed? She puffed out a breath and turned her attention back to Alvin. "I am glad your story has turned out so well. It's good of you to be out here to help."

"I would like to get back to work as much as the next person. I believe I am driving my wife crazy with all my extra time at home."

Cheryl grinned at him. "My dad does the same when he's home. My parents love each other, but they've decided there is a thing called 'too much together time.'"

Levi looked at the dwindling pile of cut lumber. "The men are putting the walls up faster than we are cutting."

Taking the cue, Cheryl picked up the cooler and headed back to the tent. When she arrived, she set the now-empty cooler down and then went to Naomi. "Have I done something to offend Levi?"

"That is a question you should ask him."

Cheryl puffed out a sigh as she sat. "He just seems so prickly right now."

"All will be well. A key is to keep talking. Many of life's misunderstandings can be resolved if you just talk about them."

Cheryl knew her advice was sound, but that didn't mean it was an easy thing to do. "All right, I will try to do that."

"Wait for a time he is not tired, and it will work even better. Levi sometimes requires a slow drawing out."

"Thank you, Naomi. I am so grateful for your friendship."

The men came through for a late lunch, and the tent buzzed with the sounds of conversation and refilling the food table. What had looked like an overwhelming pile of food had all but disappeared half an hour after the first man walked into the tent.

Lisa Troyer arrived and met her father, who had been supervising the work. The two went from table to table, stopping to thank each man who had stopped to spend the day working for them. Cheryl overheard her telling more than one person, "We couldn't have done this without you." The men seemed to appreciate the personalized thank-yous, even though Cheryl knew they would have stayed without them.

There was a small pause as they approached the last table. It was like everyone there held their breath to see what would happen. Lisa and her father approached a man with a full beard who carried himself with a regal air. Everyone's eyes were on the threesome, but Cheryl didn't recognize the man.

Cheryl leaned toward Naomi. "Who's that?"

"Teddy Harris. He is growing the beard so he looks more Amish."

"Isn't he?"

"No more than you. His factory is in Amish country, so it is Amish cheese." The woman shrugged. "What does it matter? The workers are primarily Amish, and the milk is. If he wants to wear a beard, who are we to stop him?"

"Why is he here?"

"To help, like everyone else. He wants the community to help him if it is ever needed. To do so, he needs to be part of the solution too."

The exchange between Teddy and Mr. Dauwalder was cordial. When they were done with their thank-you rounds, Lisa came to Cheryl, Naomi, and the other women. "Thank you for your part in this."

"We haven't done much." Cheryl felt like she'd done next to nothing compared to the constant activity from the men.

"Without the food, they wouldn't stay."

Naomi and Almina grinned. "Our men like their food."

Almina agreed. "That is very true. As long as there is food, they are unstoppable."

"And I am grateful." Lisa leaned against Cheryl's shoulder for a moment. "If we could find the cultures, today would be perfect." She sighed. "It's hard to believe that someone who stole them could have taken proper care of them all this time, but I want to believe. We've already seen a miracle with the building being salvageable."

Naomi squeezed her in a side hug. "Gott never leaves us. Even when we cannot always see His hand in the moment."

"We are seeing that for sure."

"Don't lose hope about the cultures." Cheryl also wanted to believe those could still be held in a protected spot.

"Oddly, I do feel better that the cultures weren't destroyed in the fire. At least this way there is still a chance that we can find them. Well, I need to go find my dad and see what's next on his list. Thank you again, ladies."

Cheryl talked with the gals for a few minutes then went to her car to get the water. When she returned, she gave everyone a hug. "I'll head back to the Swiss Miss, but if you need anything just call."

Chief Twitchell turned into the parking lot as she headed back to her car. She waited for him. "Hi, Chief."

"Cheryl. How are you today?"

"Great. What brings you out here?"

"Teddy Harris. He had a question for me." The chief stretched his back. "I wanted to see the progress too. Looks like they've done a lot."

"They've barely stopped all day." Cheryl put on her most beguiling smile. "Do you mind if I come with you?"

"Cheryl."

"I promise I won't say anything."

"All right. Come on."

Teddy Harris stopped the moment he saw them coming and stood in front of them. "Thanks for coming, Chief. I don't think this will take long."

"No problem. What can I help you with?"

"I got an e-mail from someone who wanted to sell me some cultures. He wouldn't tell me more, but it made me think it could be related to the theft here."

"Do you have the e-mail?"

"Sure. I can forward it to you."

"Good. Then we can try to trace it back to the sender."

"I've already done some of that. It's an unregistered mobile device from near Sugarcreek. Here's the important thing." Teddy leaned closer to the chief. "Whoever it was says he has buyers out of the country if I'm not interested. I hope that he's caught before he tries to leave the country with those cultures. If not transported correctly, they'll never survive the trip."

The chief took a few more notes then met Teddy's gaze. "I'll call the Internet company to see where the e-mail came from. Maybe we'll find somethin' you can't. Thanks for the information. If he contacts you again, let me know and try to stall him."

"Will do."

Cheryl followed Chief Twitchell back to the parking lot. "This sounds like a good lead."

"Yes. The strongest one we have at the moment. I'd love to close this case."

As Cheryl headed to her car and took one last look at the construction and the walls that were almost up, more than anything she wanted this lead to be the one that closed the mystery.

Chapter Twenty-Eight

"Cheryl, can you help me a moment?" Naomi's voice stopped Cheryl right before she climbed into her car.

"Sure." She closed the car door. "What do you need?"

"I need to get all these dishes and pans into the buggy."

Cheryl hurried over to help her friend. After they put that load into the buggy, they headed to the tent to grab more. It took two trips to get everything loaded into the storage space in the buggy.

"Thank you for your help. It would have been much more work if I did the job alone." Naomi slid everything around a bit more to make it secure. "Okay, we are good."

"I'll come back to make sure there isn't anything else."

When they reached the tent, Jessica Mast was being hugged by Almina, who looked up at them with a sad expression. "They have signed a contract to sell their farm."

Naomi hurried over and joined the hug. "I am so sorry, Jessica."

"There was nothing more we could do. I feel so bad that everyone helped us rebuild and now we have to sell after all."

Cheryl wanted to join the hug but held back and let the women who best knew Jessica comfort her. "Who did you sell to?"

Jessica pulled back, her shoulders rounded. "Elliott. He's going to visit family for Christmas—flying out today—but he'll be back in mid-January to finish the paperwork."

"Elliott?" Cheryl frowned at his name. "Do you mean Elliott Lawson?"

"Ja, Elliott Lawson from the Lawson company. He wanted the property years ago, but we changed our minds. Refused to sell to him. He was furious at the time. It scared me. But with the fire and now loss of business, well, we can no longer afford it."

"But if he can't come back until mid-January, Heini's will be back in business."

"Myron said we cannot wait. The bank wants too much from us now. We can buy time by showing them we have a buyer." She shrank even more. "It seems so unfair. I have never dreamed of raising our family anywhere but where we are."

Naomi squeezed her arm. "Gott has a plan."

"I know He does, but it is very hard to imagine what it is right now."

Cheryl tuned out of the conversation for a moment because something Jessica had said bothered her. "What was the man's name again?"

"Elliott Lawson."

Cheryl shook her head, and her stomach sank. "How didn't I see it before?"

"See what?"

"That Elliott Lawson was the man I saw on e-Love. He spends a couple weeks every Christmas in Europe with his family. And he's the same Elliott Lawson who works for Lawson Development and wants to bring that development to Sugarcreek."

"You know him?"

"No, but he came up on a profile search my mom had me look at. Only it didn't use his whole name. Just his first name. Still, I should have known from the photos alone."

Jessica looked disinterested. "It does not matter. He will buy our farm, and we will move."

"But it could. What if he's creating an environment where you have to sell?"

"It does not matter. What is done is settled."

"But it doesn't have to be." Cheryl knew something was more wrong than just the fact he wanted to buy the farm. Developers did that by definition, and why would the profile on e-Love matter? She grabbed her cell phone and pulled up Chief Twitchell's number.

Naomi stepped closer and looked at the phone. "Why are you calling him?"

"I'm afraid Elliott Lawson is preparing to leave the country with the remaining cheese cultures. He knows five cultures won't be enough for Heini's to reopen, but if the others are discovered, they could come back from what's essentially a delay." She waited as the phone rang. "If I'm wrong, okay. But I can't stand the thought that we could have stopped him if I'm correct."

"Hello?"

"Chief Twitchell, how far are you from the airport?"

"The Akron/Canton airport?"

"Yes, I suppose."

"Why?"

"I think Elliott Lawson is leaving the country with the rest of the cheese cultures."

"From Heini's?"

"Yes. He has the most to gain in a crazy way." She took a breath. "When Teddy Harris told you about the e-mails, that made him less of a suspect. And Lawson has been taking advantage of the farmers potentially being in distress with Heini's closing. Jessica Mast just told us they are selling to Lawson when he gets back in town. And Billy McCullar told me that the man who hired him to burn the Masts' barn also wanted him to torch Heini's but he said no."

"Whoa. Wait a minute, Cheryl. Billy told you that?"

"Yesterday. He promised to tell you by today, and if he didn't, I told him I would."

"So you think Lawson is behind all of this?"

"I do. Maybe he expected their barn burning to encourage the Masts to sell. And then when it didn't, he got creative. Maybe he thought that if he hit Heini's in a way they couldn't recover that the Masts would sell. It's working."

"It's all circumstantial, Cheryl."

"Maybe, but if you get him at the airport before he leaves, I'm certain you'll find he has the cultures." Cheryl knew all the connections were coming together. "Remember Teddy told you that in the e-mail the man said he had another buyer lined up in another country? It all makes sense. How many people in this area have connections in Europe and make regular trips there?"

"It's not that hard, Cheryl."

"It would take another cheese maker to understand the culture's value."

"Lawson isn't a cheese maker."

"But he wants the land. This is one step closer to getting it. In fact, his plan is working."

"You don't know that for sure." Chief Twitchell sounded exasperated as he huffed out the words.

"But if we don't check and I am right, the cultures will be gone forever. And there are cheese makers around here he could talk to, to understand the process. It doesn't take much research online to figure out that the cultures are a key part of cheese making." Cheryl sighed. The chances of catching Lawson slipped away with each moment she had to spend convincing the chief. Once he was on the plane, the cultures would never be recovered. "Please check."

"Why wouldn't it be a petty theft? Or someone who wants to get rid of competition?"

"It could be except you've already found alibis for Mr. Byler, Teddy Harris, and Mr. Collins." Cheryl tried to think of a fresh argument that would sway him. "It all comes back to the development. Lawson Development is in trouble and needs a project that works." The article about the lack of projects and Ben Vogel's comment about banks not wanting to loan the company money came to her. She put the chief on speaker so she could navigate to the article. When she found it, she moved away from the people milling around and read it to him, finishing with, "This article mentions the company's money problems."

The chief paused a moment as if thinking then said, "All right. I'll see if I can talk to him."

"Thank you." She switched her phone off the speaker mode.

"Start prayin' you're right because otherwise I'm going to have some explaining to do."

As she climbed into her vehicle and drove away, Cheryl had no problem doing exactly what he suggested. She wanted nothing more than for God to shine light on who had orchestrated the theft and fire. And if the cultures were discovered in the process, all the better. Then there was a fighting chance Lisa and her father could save them and use them to relaunch Heini's.

All the chief had to do was find Elliott Lawson and confirm whether he had the critical cheese cultures.

CHAPTER TWENTY-NINE

By the time she returned to Sugarcreek, Lydia and Esther had cleaned the Swiss Miss and were ready to leave for the evening. The store looked ready for the last week of shopping before Christmas Eve. The displays of candles, games, and other Amish delights were replenished and arranged in attractive displays. The floor looked like it had been freshly swept and mopped, and the faint scent of pine and cinnamon hung in the air as if a candle or two had been lit. Even the candy bins were refilled and new ornaments hung on display in a decorative pattern.

"It looks great. Thanks, you two." Cheryl's throat clenched with emotion as she thought of how well these two had grown into their roles at the Swiss Miss. Both had been younger teens when they started, and now Cheryl could leave them in charge with confidence they could handle any questions that came their way.

Esther's eyes sparkled as she finished pulling on gloves. "It is a pleasure to help here."

"A privilege," Lydia added. "Danki for letting me work here."

Cheryl hugged them both and tried to think up an appropriate Christmas present for the girls as she watched them leave the store.

She wanted to let them know in a tangible way just how much she appreciated them. Maybe she'd get them gift certificates to the Berryhills' bookstore. Then they could each get books that they liked to read. That would be perfect.

An hour went by as Cheryl caught up on paperwork. It would make her life much easier when she returned from her trip home for Christmas if she were as caught up as possible, but the paperwork wasn't her favorite part of managing the store. Still, it was an important aspect of the job.

Beau meowed loudly and then stretched up to paw at her pant leg. When that didn't pull her attention, he hopped into her lap. Cheryl laughed as she gently set him down. "Not yet, boy." She glanced at the pile of papers left. "I need more time to finish this."

The Siamese remained undeterred as he reached up again and this time let her feel his claws.

"Beau!" She batted him down more firmly, and he slinked to the corner and sat there primly grooming his front paws and then his face. "I'm sorry, but I need a bit more time."

Another hour passed before Cheryl looked up and realized she hadn't really accomplished much. Her thoughts kept straying to Elliott Lawson and whether she was right about him. Had he been behind the cheese culture theft? Was he the man who ordered Billy to burn the Masts' barn? And hired someone else to destroy Heini's? Part of her didn't want to think this way about someone she barely knew, but she had learned that greed could be a powerful motive for people to do the unthinkable.

If Lawson Development was desperate for a successful new project, that could be sufficient to make Elliott take a jaunt down an illegal path.

It certainly wouldn't be the last time a businessman found himself at a crossroads choosing the wrong path.

The bigger question was if he was the thief, had he taken sufficient care of the delicate cultures that they could be salvaged and used by the Dauwalders as they rebuilt Heini's? Cheryl prayed that was the case, but it seemed like that would take an incredible miracle for it to occur.

"God, I know You are able." She spoke the words into the empty space of the office. Her shoulders slumped, and she slid lower in the chair. "While You're in the miracle business, could you help me understand what's happening with Levi? I'll admit I'm so confused. Being honest about our feelings was supposed to make things between us easier. It's had the opposite impact."

She lowered her head and just waited in the stillness of the office.

She'd learned a long time ago that God could speak to her wherever she was. He didn't care about the address as much as He cared about the sensitivity of her heart toward Him. She needed Him to guide and direct this relationship because if He wasn't in it, she didn't want to be either. No relationship was worth risking her connection with God.

"All right, Beau. Let's head home."

When Beau was in his carrier and she had bundled up, Cheryl took one more pass through the store, confirming everything was turned off and ready for the morning. Then she set the security alarm, hefted Beau's carrier and her purse, and headed out the front door. The bell dinged outside as she set the carrier down and locked the door. Behind her on the street she could hear the stamp of horses' hooves and the jingle of bells. Someone was getting their buggy into the Christmas spirit.

It didn't matter. The buggy owner she cared about had given no indication he wanted to find her for a special buggy ride in the snow. She'd even wondered if he'd take her out in the sleigh, but that hadn't occurred either. Last winter when they'd been friends only, she would have easily asked him, and he probably would have agreed. This winter? Surely his answer would be a quick no. A knee-jerk reaction to avoid any hint of a romantic moment.

"Cheryl, how long are you going to stand at the door?" Levi's strong, rich voice tugged her gaze around.

"Levi?"

He looked wonderful in his heavy coat, hat pulled over his ears, scarf wrapped tightly around his neck. Sugar stamped his feet and seemed to eye Cheryl as if to ask what was taking so long.

"What are you doing here?"

"I thought I would give you a ride home if you are willing. Esther mentioned you walked."

Cheryl nodded. "I did. When I returned from Millersburg, there wasn't a place to park near the store. So I parked at home and walked. But even in winter it seems silly to drive just a few blocks."

"Seems silly to carry that cat back and forth."

She mock frowned at him and held Beau's carrier in front of her body in a firm hold. "Beau belongs at the Swiss Miss every bit as much as I do."

Levi held up a hand as if to stop the flow of words and let the other loosely hold the reins. "I did not want to start an argument. I would drive. That is all." He looked at her with a hint of longing in his eyes. "Can I drive you home?"

Cheryl tried to read his thoughts, but failed miserably. Finally, her teeth started to chatter, and she nodded. "Thank you."

"My pleasure." Levi hopped down and took Beau from her. Then he helped her into the buggy before reclaiming Beau's carrier and setting it in the back. He lithely hopped into the buggy, settled a lap blanket around her, and then with a click, Sugar began to trot down the street.

Silence settled over them, perfect for the frosty winter night, but a silence that left Cheryl wondering what had changed. Levi left his gaze on the road, yet his posture was relaxed, the reins hanging loosely in his grip, Sugar free to follow his head down Main. Cheryl glanced at the road then back at Levi. She did that a couple times before she tugged the blanket more snuggly around her.

Should she say something, break the peace of the moment, or should she ask him why his response had changed? It was unexpected, and she would like an explanation. It felt a bit like she'd been whipsawed by his fairly cold treatment earlier in the week to showing up tonight with a romantic buggy ride. At least Cheryl wanted it to be romantic, but hesitated to let herself believe it. What if his feelings changed again? Would she be able to protect her heart if she kept letting him in close?

Levi clucked and tugged on one rein, guiding Sugar to turn on to the road that led to Cheryl's home. Then he looked at her with a relaxed grin. "You might as well say it."

Cheryl opened her mouth then closed it. Uncertainty gurgled through her.

He nudged her shoulder with his. A wave of heat traveled down her arm. "I'm listening."

She opened her mouth and then nodded. "Okay. I don't understand why you were so distant this week. You seemed so far away from me even when we were in the same place."

He shook his head and then sighed. "I know it does not make sense. And I am sorry if I hurt you." He shifted against the buggy seat then looked at her. "Cheryl, I was afraid you would change your mind about me, about us. It is one thing to feel what has grown between us and know it is nothing more than a dream. It is something very different to know that it could be."

His words rippled through her. "You're afraid too."

"Ja."

The simple word bridged the pain that his distance had caused. She could understand his fears because she wrestled with similar. She leaned her head against his shoulder. "I wish this were easier."

"If it were, it would not mean as much. There is something about the journey, the wrestling, that makes the process valuable." He sighed. "All I know with certainty, Cheryl, is that no other woman has captured my thoughts the way you do."

"Not even Emma?"

"No." Levi slowed Sugar as Cheryl's home came into view. "Will you forgive me for walking in fear?"

Cheryl closed her eyes, not wanting to see how close the cottage was. She longed to capture this moment and extend it before life intervened. It would be nice to pretend that if she just kept her eyes closed, she could live in a dream where Levi's feelings for her weren't conflicted. Instead, she sat up and returned his gaze in the light of the street lamp. "I will. Please forgive me too. I was afraid you had changed your mind about us." She exhaled a laugh. "I guess we were both afraid the other would change."

Levi wrapped an arm around her shoulder, and she sank against him. This felt so right. She would need to continue to pray about what direction God wanted to take their friendship, but Cheryl had no desire to explore other relationships. This time her mom wasn't right. This was a friendship worth the time. She'd trust God with the ending.

CHAPTER THIRTY

The cottage felt small as Cheryl watched Levi pull away. Joy radiated through her chest, a feeling she would savor.

Her heart felt full and warm at the time she'd just spent with Levi. It had been so thoughtful of him to bring her home and give them some much-needed time to reconnect. Beau scratched to be let out, so she set his carrier down and released him. He stretched his front legs forward then his back legs before strutting down the hall to the kitchen. Cheryl hung her coat and then sank on to the couch. She should make supper. It was already late for a meal. Instead, she settled herself to remember their conversation and pray.

If she truly wanted God's best for her life, then she needed to ask Him to show her what that was.

Cheryl spent a few moments resting and praying then stood and headed to the kitchen. She started the water to boil tortellini and heat spaghetti sauce, then she pulled out the rest of her Christmas presents. Hopefully she'd finish wrapping tonight, and then a couple more days at the Swiss Miss, Christmas morning with the Millers, and then the flight to Seattle for Christmas with her family. It would feel good to get this item checked off her to-do list.

She had eaten and then gathered all the trappings to wrap the presents when her cell phone rang. She set the long tubes of wrapping paper to the side and then grabbed a roll of gold curling ribbon that threatened to tumble off of the counter before she glanced at her phone. The screen didn't show a number that she recognized, but since she hadn't heard back from the chief about Elliott Lawson, she answered anyway.

"Hello?"

"Cheryl, this is Lisa. Lisa Troyer." The woman's voice was rushed and ecstatic. "You're never going to believe what has happened."

From her tone, Cheryl wasn't sure if Lisa was happy, upset, or stunned. "Is everything all right?"

"Yes." Now Cheryl could hear tears in her friend's voice. "The cultures. The chief just brought them out to Heini's."

"Are they okay?"

"Yes. It literally feels like a miracle. I had braced myself for the worst. Either they were gone, or they'd been in the wrong hands for long enough that they were as good as gone. Instead, he brought them to us in a couple coolers." She took a shuddering breath. "Cheryl, it looks like they've been refrigerated the whole time. We'll need to do some checking, but so far they all look usable."

"Heini's can rise from the ashes."

"Yes! That's exactly what it feels like. Everything looked so bleak just a week ago. It looked like the factory would need to be rebuilt. Instead it was just a wall and part of the roof. We still need to clean and sanitize, but that's very doable."

"Oh, Lisa. I am so glad."

"Cheryl, this wouldn't have happened without your help. You were the one who put everything together."

"What do you mean?"

"That's what Chief Twitchell told me. I know he's worked hard on this case, but he gave you the credit for knowing that Elliott Lawson was behind everything." Lisa choked back a sob then cleared her throat. "Cheryl, if they hadn't gotten the cultures when they did, they would have been destroyed in the flight. He might have managed to care for them since the fire, but that was about to end. I . . . we . . . we don't know how to repay you."

"There's nothing you need to do. I'm glad I could help." And she wanted to talk to Chief Twitchell and hear from him what had happened.

"At a minimum you'll enjoy Heini's cheese for life."

"I'm so glad it will be back in stores. You know I love the pimento one."

"We'll keep you in a lifetime supply. Truly, thank you."

Cheryl assured her it was her pleasure then let Lisa go so her excited friend could tell more people the good news. The moment the call ended, Cheryl called Chief Twitchell. "Sir, I think you forgot to tell me something."

Chief Twitchell chuckled. "Not a bit. Just haven't had a chance to call. We had a suspect to book first."

"So it was Elliott?"

"Looks that way, though we will continue to investigate. Right now we have him for possession of stolen property. The rest remains to be seen. The theft charge is enough to keep him here for a bit while we look for more evidence."

"He had the cultures?"

"He did. Looks like he stumbled into properly keeping them. Lisa Troyer seemed pretty relieved. Sounds like Elliott didn't know what he was doin' and got lucky that he didn't destroy the cultures. I guess she'll know for sure once Heini's restarts cheese production, but everything looks good so far."

Cheryl didn't fight the smile that started stretching her face. "That is wonderful news."

"It is. I'm glad you pulled the pieces together, though I'm still a little unclear on how you did. And I'm still not sold on the arson, but I have a feelin' we'll prove that too before we're done."

"Talk to Billy McCullar. He'll help you on the arson."

"Already am. Well, I need to get home to the ever-patient missus."

"Thanks for the update."

As Cheryl looked at the presents left to wrap, a great sense of peace settled over her. She could now focus on finishing preparation for Christmas because all was well for her friends and Heini's would reopen.

It was a great feeling, and one she didn't want to forget on an evening filled with happy endings.

CHAPTER THIRTY-ONE

Cheryl parked her car in front of the Millers' home, taking in the sight of candles flickering in the windowsills and movement beyond the windows. Just a few weeks ago it had been hard to imagine a simple, happy Christmas with so much happening with the fire at Heini's, but now everything had changed. Elliott Lawson had officially been charged with theft and arson, and Billy McCullar had been charged with a lesser charge and was currently in a work release program. Knowing that Heini's would be up and running in full in just a matter of months had convinced the Mast family—and others—not to sell their farms. And in addition to the gifts that Cheryl had gathered and provided, other families in the community had surrounded the struggling farmers and given enough for them to make it through the coming months.

And added to all that, a smile touched Cheryl's lips knowing that all was right between her and Levi—or at least as right as it could be at this time. They both cared for each other, that she knew. And she trusted that the Lord would lead them to the right type of relationship in His time.

Cheryl carried a bag of gifts and a plate of her favorite cookies and walked up to the Millers' house before knocking on the front door. The door opened, and Esther welcomed her in, the cadence of the young woman's dialect causing Cheryl to smile.

"We've been waiting for you, all of us have. We have *wunderbar* good things planned...especially Levi."

Cheryl's heartbeat quickened as she scanned the room, looking for him. She didn't see him, and she tried to hide her disappointment. Her eyes met Naomi's, and she couldn't miss the note of disappointment there. Was it because Sarah and her husband would not be joining them this year? Cheryl guessed it would be hard not to have one of your children home at Christmas. Did Naomi ever worry that Levi would follow in Sarah's footsteps? If she ever did, Cheryl never saw hint of it, especially with the way the older woman playfully teased her concerning Levi.

"Levi is out in the buggy shed. He should be in before long," Naomi said, as if answering Cheryl's silent question. "And let me give you a hand with those things. It was so nice of you to come. And...I have to show you your first gift." Naomi chuckled, and with her laughter the disappointment in her gaze slipped away. "This gift, well, it is much too big to hide."

Naomi took the plate of cookies from her hand and hustled into the kitchen. Cheryl set her bag of gifts on a side table, which held a few other wrapped packages. Then she followed Naomi into the kitchen. Unlike most English homes there was no tree, there were no piles of presents or gaudy decorations, but the spirit of the holiday was just as alive in this home as in any Cheryl had ever been in. Wonderful smells of cooking food wafted through the house, and there was a lightness to the air. An open Bible rested on the kitchen table—opened to Luke chapter two—and Cheryl guessed that story of Christ's birth would be the center of their celebration, as it should be.

Then with a grin and a swoop of her hand, Naomi motioned to the largest gift basket Cheryl had ever seen. It was a large wicker basket, and it was filled with cheese. Large rounds of cheese, small packages of cheese, and cheese spread in all types of flavors. And all of them bore the name Heini's. It was as if someone had taken the remaining stock at Swissters and had piled it into a basket.

Laughter spilled from Cheryl's mouth at the sight of it. "What in the world?"

"Lisa Troyer brought the basket over just an hour ago. She guessed you'd be joining us for Christmas. And Lisa says that whenever this runs out you know where to find more."

"More? I can imagine." Cheryl chuckled again. "Grilled cheese sandwiches are one thing I know how to cook. I'm set for life."

As Cheryl stepped forward to take a peek at the different varieties, the door behind her opened and a voice boomed out.

"I know this may sound *cheesy*, but Cheryl, are you ready for your second gift of the day?"

Cheryl turned and eyed Levi standing in the doorway. He took a step in, glanced down at his snow-covered, dirty boots, and then grinned at Naomi. "Instead of me coming in and muddying up the floor, would you mind joining me outside? Meet me in the buggy shed. I have a surprise for you."

"A surprise? What could be better than cheese?" she teased.

The door shut again, and Cheryl turned to her friend. "You've trained him well."

Naomi wrinkled her nose as she smiled. "Are you talking about not messing up my clean floor, the lame joke, or having a surprise for you?" She laughed. "Because I had nothing to do with the last two but plenty of complaints that led to the first one."

"Not messing up the floor, of course!"

Since Cheryl hadn't taken off her coat yet, she tucked her scarf tighter around her neck and then hurried toward the buggy shed. A blanket of dull gray clouds filled the sky, but it did nothing to hinder her bright spirits. As she turned the corner to the shed, Cheryl paused and gasped. The buggy's wheels were gone, and they had been replaced with sled runners. More than that, the buggy had been decorated with thousands of twinkling white lights.

"Levi, it looks like something Cinderella would ride in!"

He smiled. "I know that is a fairy tale character, and that was my gift to you tonight—to make you feel as if you were part of a fairy tale of your own. It appears as if I am off to a goot start." He extended his gloved hand, and she approached, placing her hand in his.

"Yes, Levi. I agree with you. You're off to a good start indeed."

She climbed into the buggy, and Levi tucked a lap blanket around her. Then he settled in for the ride. With a flick of the reins the horse headed out, and as if ordered up in order to create the perfect moment, a soft snow fluttered from the sky.

"Levi, it's just perfect."

"Ja, I am glad you think so. Just look around and take it in."

"It?"

"The scenery of course. What belongs...and maybe what does not."

Cheryl wasn't sure what he meant, but after a few minutes she noticed a small sign tacked to the fence post. It read: Sweet.

She pointed. "I'm not sure I've seen that before. What does it mean?"

Levi glanced over at her and shrugged. "Keep watching."

Not too much farther, there was another sign. This one read: Kind. As they continued on, she spotted more signs with words on the fence posts: Selfless, Considerate, Humble, Beautiful. The last word made Cheryl blush.

"So you guessed that I was talking about you...about your qualities."

"I was hoping."

Levi cleared his throat. He ran a finger under his collar as if suddenly embarrassed. "Sometimes the best gift we can give a person is a small trinket, but as I thought about it, I decided that what I wanted to give you was a reflection of what you already have and who you already are."

Tears rimmed Cheryl's eyes. Happy tears. "Thank you, Levi. I don't know what to say."

He stopped the buggy and then turned in his seat to face her. "I know what you can say. Please, Cheryl, say that you will stick with me, even when I let fear get ahold of my heart, even when I question the future or feel confused."

She nodded. "Yes, I'll stick with you, Levi. I promise I will."

He released a big breath, as if he'd been holding it for a while. "It is a beautiful day then, for the Dauwalder family, for the Mast and other Amish families, and for us."

"A new beginning is a beautiful thing," she offered with a sigh. And then Cheryl stretched out her hand and watched the soft snowflakes fall on to her mitten. "Just as this day celebrates Christ giving us a new beginning with His birth, I'm thankful for all the ways He comes into our hearts and guides us to helping and loving and serving just as He did."

"He did not have to do it for us, Cheryl," Levi added. "But I suppose that is what love is all about. Giving because you want to and caring even though it is not required."

Love. It was a beautiful word. Love, she knew, was something as pure and beautiful as the twinkling lights, but something that also could be as gentle and unassuming as the falling snow. And even though some people found love by seeking it out, she was thankful it had come to her in unexpected ways. She didn't know what the future held for her and Levi, but with the first roots of love, their relationship was something that could be built on one tender moment like this at a time. And believing in that was the greatest gift of all.

Author Letter

Dear Reader,

I remember the first time I stepped into Heini's Cheese Chalet. I was in Holmes County for a book signing, and my friend Lisa Troyer met me at the door with a huge grin. She showed me around the store, and I enjoyed the numerous samples of delicious cheese. Then an elderly guide told us about the cheese-making process. Through large windows we were able to peek into the production area and watch an Amish gentleman stirring curds and separating the whey. It was fascinating to watch! Here's a summary of what I learned:

Lisa's grandfather, John (Hans) Dauwalder, trained as a master cheese maker in Switzerland and came to the United States in the 1920s to display his artisan talents in a growing cheese market. After several successful years at the Bunker Hill Cheese Co-op, John decided to return to his hometown in Switzerland to further his romance with Lili Mueller. The two fell in love and were married in 1933.

In 1948, John and Lili, together with their two children, Peter (Lisa's father) and Marguerite (her aunt), sold the family farm in Switzerland to join John's brother Crist in the United States. Crist had purchased Bunker Hill Cheese in 1935 and asked John to join him in building the family cheese business.

In 1962, Lisa's parents, Peter and Nancy, who were married in 1955, acquired Bunker Hill Cheese. The name was changed to Heini, a short version of Heinrich, a typical Swiss name that shows their heritage. Today, it is one of the premier cheese retailers east of the Mississippi River and one of the most successful wholesale manufacturers serving clients throughout North America.

The family business continues to be the primary outlet for the Amish farms in the region. If you ever find yourself near Sugarcreek, Ohio, be sure to stop by to watch the Amish work and try the yummy samples! Like me, you won't be disappointed.

Tricia Goyer

About the Authors

Best-selling author Tricia Goyer has published fifty books and more than five hundred articles! She is a two-time Carol Award winner as well as a Christy and ECPA Award nominee. In 2010, she was selected as one of the "Top Twenty Moms to Follow on Twitter" by SheKnows.com. Tricia blogs at ForTheFamily.com, TheBetterMom.com, and NotQuiteAmishLiving.com. She is a mother of six, grandmother of two, and wife to John, and they make their home in Little Rock, Arkansas. To learn more, visit TriciaGoyer.com.

Cara Putman is a homeschooling mom of four who is married to the love of her life. An award-winning author, Cara has published more than twenty books and is an attorney and lecturer at Purdue University. She blogs at TheGroveStory.com, InspiredByLifeAndFiction.com, TheWritersAlleyBlog.com, and CaraPutman.com and serves on the executive board of American Christian Fiction Writers, which is a great resource for anyone who longs to write.

Fun Fact about
the Amish or Sugarcreek, Ohio

All around Sugarcreek many Amish families are setting up their own businesses, and smaller businesses, government offices, and others who want to draw in Amish customers do all they can to accommodate Amish transportation. Hitching posts up front make them buggy friendly. Like many businesses near Sugarcreek, Heini's Cheese Chalet has a hitching post in their parking lot for Amish buggies.

Also, among those Amish communities that allow bicycles, many church members often ride their bikes to the store. Road signs warn about the presence of buggies along the country roads and highways.

Around the county, both hitching posts and bike racks can be found at grocery stores, fabric stores, and even at McDonald's. Of course if the Amish don't want to go inside to eat their Big Macs, buggies are also often found passing through the drive-up window line.

Something Delicious from Our Sugarcreek Friends

Wedding Potatoes

9 large potatoes, peeled and
   cubed

6 ounces cream cheese

1 cup sour cream

1 teaspoon salt

2 teaspoons onion salt

¼ teaspoon ground black
   pepper

2 tablespoons butter

½ cup American cheese

Cook potatoes in a large kettle with salted water until tender. Drain water. To the potatoes, add cream cheese, sour cream, salt, onion salt, pepper, butter, and cheese. Mash until smooth. Put into greased nine-by-thirteen-inch casserole dish and bake, covered, for thirty minutes at 350 degrees.

A SPECIAL GIFT FOR GUIDEPOSTS READERS!

Lisa Troyer, the owner of Heini's Cheese Chalet, the cheese factory that is featured in *Blessed Are the Cheese Makers*, has graciously provided Guideposts readers of Sugarcreek Amish Mysteries with a free collection of original Christmas music, written and performed by her and Dawn Yoder. To gain access to these downloadable tracks in mp3 format, simply go to merrychristmassongs.com and prepare to be blessed!

Read on for a sneak peek of another exciting book
in the series Sugarcreek Amish Mysteries!

Stranger Things Have Happened
by Amy Lillard

Thank you, and come again." Cheryl Cooper handed the bag
across the counter to the plump, grandmotherly tourist.

"My name's Peggy." The woman smiled, her cherub cheeks
rosy. "I will be back. I sure will," she said. "This is just the nicest
shop." She took the bag and, with one last beaming smile, turned
to leave the Swiss Miss Gifts and Sundries shop.

It was three o'clock on Wednesday afternoon. Hump day in
January. The beginning of the countdown to the weekend. Not
that Cheryl was really counting down. Especially since the weekend
promised more of the same gray skies and slushy, dirty snow. She'd
been in Sugarcreek a year and a half now, and she prayed she'd be
able to stay for years to come. She loved Sugarcreek, even in gray
January. She also loved managing the Swiss Miss. Accepting the
job of supervising her aunt Mitzi's store and moving from
Columbus to Sugarcreek when Mitzi moved to Papua New Guinea
to do mission work had been a dramatic change in Cheryl's life.
Now she couldn't imagine doing anything else. Hopefully, her
aunt would allow Cheryl to stay on, maybe even sell the store to

Cheryl, even if she should decide someday to return from the mission field to Sugarcreek.

Cheryl smiled and gave a little wave to Peggy when she called good-bye near the door. Her winter coat made shushing noises as she walked.

But it was nothing compared to the sound that erupted outside. Well, not really erupted, but grew and grew until it took over every little noise inside the Swiss Miss.

"What is going on out there?" Lydia asked.

Esther stopped dusting shelves and restocking pot holders to look at Cheryl, the question in her eyes so obvious.

"I don't know." Cheryl walked around the counter and started toward the door. The sound was getting louder and louder and sounded an awful lot like . . .

"Oh my," Peggy gasped. She stopped, still in the Swiss Miss, though her hand was on the doorknob. "I've never seen anything like that."

Cheryl stared out the window, scarcely believing what she saw.

"They're pigs!" Lydia exclaimed.

Hundreds of them. Dirty pigs, clean pigs, Saddleback, solid-colored, all with quirky little tails and running pell-mell down the street.

"Excuse me." Cheryl nudged her way in front of Peggy who now showed no signs of leaving the Swiss Miss. Not that Cheryl could blame her. She wasn't really excited about walking into a street full of pigs. But the sight was so phenomenal she couldn't stop herself.

If she thought the noise was loud inside, it was nothing compared to outside. Running feet, squealing swine, and the tremble of hooves on the pavement.

"Get together and make a barricade," someone called.

Cheryl sprang into action at the call for help and joined hands with those on either side of her, along with several other merchants and residents and even a few tourists. They created a barrier across the street. The pigs skidded to a halt, tumbling on top of themselves and squealing as they turned around to run in the other direction. Cars honked as the beasts took off down side roads. Traffic was at a standstill, understandable considering the fact that the road was filled with pigs.

"What happened?" Cheryl asked. She looked to her left, only then noticing that she held hands with Kathy Kimble from the Honey Bee.

The blonde-haired café owner shook her head then winced as the pigs ran up to her then flopped over backward in their attempts to go the other direction. "A transport truck turned over just on the other side of town. At least that's what they're saying."

That explained why there were so many pigs. How many would one of those trucks hold anyway?

"I'm not sure this is working," Cheryl said as a small pig ran between their legs.

The man on her right nodded.

Cheryl had never seen him before but could only assume that he was in town visiting. He was fair-skinned with green eyes, light brown hair, and a gaze that seemed to soak up everything around him. "They're just going back in the other direction," he commented.

Kathy shook her head. "I am not chasing pigs down the street."

"I don't blame you." And definitely not in this weather. It was cold, cold, *cold* outside, not good weather for chasing pigs. Or much else for that matter. Cheryl shivered. She should have grabbed her coat, but who had time for that?

Just then the police chief, Sam Twitchell, arrived on the scene. He had to park his car on a side street, dodging pigs in the process.

Cheryl stifled a laugh. Was it really funny? Or was it the thought of the chief and a pig? She quickly sobered as he got out of his car, scowling as if he had realized the joke as well.

Cheryl remained in the street, holding the hands of a complete stranger in their barricade line, as the chief and one of his officers talked. She wished she could hear their conversation. It would be interesting to know what they were going to do with the pigs and how they planned to get them back where they belonged.

"You say they were in a transport truck?" Cheryl asked. She turned to the man next to her.

He nodded. "Yeah. It was right there in front of the car dealership. I passed it on my way in."

"What a day to visit." Cheryl laughed as pigs continued to run and squeal chaotically in the street.

"Oh, I'm not visiting. I've moved here. Daniel Rossi," he said. "Pleased to meet you. I'd shake your hand but…" He nodded at their joined hands and shrugged.

"No worries," Cheryl said. "Cheryl Cooper. I run the Swiss Miss gift shop. And this is Kathy Kimble. She owns the Honey Bee Café."

He nodded. "I've already heard about the Honey Bee. The food is supposed to be really good."

"I like to think so," Kathy said with a smile.

"I'll have to try it out soon. Like maybe as soon as they get these pigs out of the street."

"Why don't you come by tomorrow at lunch?" Kathy suggested. "It might be a little better timing."

Daniel smiled. "I'm looking forward to it."

"What brings you to town?" Cheryl asked.

"I'm a new reporter over at the tri-county newspaper, *The Gazette.*"

"That's great," Kathy said. "Good to have some different reporters around."

"Really?" Daniel said. "It doesn't seem like a lot happens around here." He looked around at the hundreds of pigs. "I mean, normally."

Cheryl laughed. "You might just be surprised."

All in all, it took two hours to get the majority of the pigs off the streets, and Cheryl was positive they had forgotten a couple. It seemed like a nearly impossible task to find every single one. Here and there, one would dart past, usually with someone following close behind.

The excitement had made foot traffic nonexistent, and Cheryl had stayed outside to watch as they loaded the pigs into the backs of personal trucks and hauled them off back down the road toward the broken-down eighteen-wheeler.

Cheryl turned back to the new reporter in town, but he wasn't there. She had thought to invite him to the Swiss Miss, maybe to try some of the fudge or to just look around. Of course if he ran a little piece in the paper about the shop… Well, that wouldn't hurt either.

"Where did he go?" she asked.

Kathy looked around. "Who? Daniel?"

"Yeah, the reporter."

Kathy shrugged. "I don't know. With all the crazy goings-on, he just seemed to disappear."

Odd. The afternoon's pig event was probably the biggest thing to happen in the town since the cheese factory burned down, and the new reporter vanished.

Cheryl shook her head. "You'll learn," she muttered to a reporter who was no longer there. "You don't walk out on a story like this." She swept one arm through the street.

Yes, most of the pigs had been gathered up and hauled back to the edge of town. But there were still a few stragglers squealing and running through alleyways. Foot traffic was picking up a bit as customers came out of the shops where they had taken refuge when the wave of pigs came through. The town's few police cars were parked at various intervals. A couple had their lights flashing, others not. The policemen themselves, along with the firemen and a few EMTs, still rushed around, trying to gather up wayward swine. Merchants had started to go back into their stores. They would stay open for another hour or so and then everyone would go home to dinner.

"He'll learn indeed," Cheryl said. Who knew when the next big thing would happen and whether it would be big enough to merit a news story? It could be as exciting as Albert Yoder being accused of selling raw milk across state lines or as ordinary as the local basketball team winning against their rival. But she wasn't about to tell the man how to do his job. She had come to love Sugarcreek and enjoyed the town so much. Some people just didn't understand what a special treasure it was to live and work here.

"There you are!" Levi Miller and his mother, Naomi, came down the street toward them. Levi always brought a smile to Cheryl's face. And lately she got to see him often, since his mother, or rather his stepmother, was her best friend. And Levi obviously looked for every opportunity he could to accompany his mother. Which meant Cheryl was smiling a lot these days.

"Here I am."

"We were at the grocery store," Naomi started, "and heard about all the pigs. We were worried about you." She nodded in Levi's direction.

Was that a flush rising into his cheeks?

Cheryl smiled. "It was something to see. I'm sorry you missed it."

"With all the animals at our farm and petting zoo, I do not mind missing out on a few pigs," Levi said.

Cheryl laughed and caught herself when she started to reach out a hand to squeeze his. Being Amish, Levi held a different perspective on behavior. Public displays of affection were not acceptable.

"I suppose so," Cheryl said, catching his blue gaze. She sighed. They had mutually admitted their feelings for one another. However, they were still navigating the minefield of how to make any relationship other than friendship work. One or both of them would need to compromise. Would she, *could* she become Amish? Could Levi ever consider leaving? Until these questions were answered, they would continue to move their relationship forward very slowly. Cheryl shook her head to close her daydream and return to the moment. "I suppose you have to get your groceries home."

"*Ja*," Naomi said. "But we wanted to check on you first. Make sure that you are all right."

"I'm as right as rain, as Aunt Mitzi would say." Cheryl smiled. "And I even got to meet the new reporter in town."

Levi looked around at what remained of the pig chaos. "New reporter and a new hamburger truck. Sugarcreek's growing and growing."

"Yes, the hamburger truck. I've seen it and have been meaning to grab lunch there sometime." She'd been catching up from the Christmas rush, inventorying everything, and so busy with all the other January chores that she hadn't had a chance to check out the large food truck parked next door. Maybe she needed to take a day off besides just Sunday. Give herself a chance to rest. She had been working very hard.

"I've heard their burgers are very good," Naomi added.

"Who said that?" Levi asked.

"Caleb came back with one a couple of days ago."

"I hear they're Muslims," Levi said.

"Muslims?" She'd never heard of Muslims in Sugarcreek, though she supposed there had to be a few. She had just never given it much thought.

"Do you think we should go over and introduce ourselves?"

Naomi's expression remained impassive, and Cheryl could only guess what was going through her head. The Amish didn't try to convert people to Jesus, but the idea of witnessing had been ingrained in Cheryl from an early age. If they were indeed Muslims, she could only hope that she could live a good example of Christianity before them. She accepted all peoples for who they were, but it was her duty to show the world what being a Christian meant. And it might be a good idea to go check out the menu, seeing as how she ate in town almost every day. She'd still never learned to cook much more than the very basics.

"I suppose so," Naomi said.

Levi nodded. "You should go introduce yourselves. I am going to get the buggy. Now that the streets are clear, I will bring it down and pick you up. Is that okay, *Maam*?"

Naomi nodded. "Ja. That would be fine."

Side by side, Cheryl and Naomi made their way over to the food truck. It was a standard truck, Cheryl supposed. A few dents and dings here and there. It was white with a red stripe down both sides. Patels' Patties was painted in red script across the side, and a matching red-and-white-striped awning sheltered customers who stood in line.

"This smells good," Cheryl said.

Naomi nodded.

Maybe if they were open for dinner, she would come here to eat. Just to give it a try.

"There's a goodly line as well." And there were several people already waiting even though it was a little early for dinner, Cheryl supposed.

"Should we wait?" Cheryl asked.

"Do you need to get back to the Swiss Miss?"

"I think the girls will be okay for a few more minutes. Are you and Levi taking Esther home tonight?"

"Ja, as soon as she is off work."

Cheryl got in line behind several other people. She might not be able to order yet, but she could still see the menu. Nothing But Burgers, the menu read. But there were a lot of them. Bacon burgers, cheeseburgers, Tex-Mex burgers, Greek burgers, chicken burgers, and more. If it could be put on a bun, it seemed the Patels had it.

"What is a black bean burger?" Naomi asked. The look on her face was enough to tell the tale of what she really thought about black bean burgers.

"Just what you think."

"A hamburger made out of black beans?"

Cheryl chuckled. "Among other things. They take black beans, mash them up, and mix them with onion and peppers and that sort of thing. They make it into a patty then grill it up like a beef hamburger."

Naomi's brow wrinkled. "And they put it on a bun?"

Cheryl nodded.

"And people eat these?"

"Yeah. You remember when we had that Kip Elliott, the environmentalist protester, here?"

"Oh yeah. When Albert's Rebekah had her baby."

"That's right. Elliot was a vegetarian, and that burger would be right up his alley."

Naomi nodded, though she didn't look convinced that a black bean burger would be suitable for anyone to eat regardless of their views on meat.

The couple in front of them moved to one side, and Naomi and Cheryl stepped up to the drop-down counter.

"Can I help you?" A beautiful dark-skinned girl tucked her straight, dark hair behind one ear and kept her pencil against her order pad.

"How is that Tex-Mex burger?" Cheryl asked. The girl's smile lit her whole face. Beautiful wasn't quite the word. Her skin was flawless and smooth. Her hair shone nearly blue, it was so black. Her eyes were bottomless with long lashes that looked as if they belonged on a camel instead of the teenage girl. "Spicy," she said.

Cheryl laughed. "I think I'll pass on that. I'll take a bacon cheeseburger."

The girl jotted it down on her notepad. "You want veggies on it?"

Cheryl nodded.

"Mustard and ketchup?"

"Mayo," Cheryl said.

The girl shook her head as if giving up trying to understand the workings of people who ate mayonnaise on hamburgers.

"Would you like something too?" she asked Naomi.

Naomi shook her head.

"Is that all then?"

Cheryl noticed she didn't have a trace of an accent, but the people behind her in the little truck who were cooking and shouting orders and details to one another held the thick rhythmic accents most associated with India.

"To go?"

"Yes, please," Cheryl said.

She gave Cheryl her total and she paid it, thankful that she had shoved a ten-dollar bill into her pocket earlier. Then Cheryl and Naomi stood to one side as they waited for Cheryl's order.

"Levi should be here any minute," Cheryl said. "As soon as he is, you can go ahead and take Esther home. I don't want you guys to wait. It might be chilly out here, but that doesn't mean your groceries will last."

"I thank you, Cheryl, but if you need Esther, we can manage."

"Here you go." The young girl held the sack toward Cheryl. She thanked her and took it then started back toward the Swiss Miss.

"That does smell good," Naomi said, giving an appreciative sniff.

"If you come into town tomorrow, I'll treat you to lunch there."

Naomi looked as if she were about to protest and gave a small nod. "I would like that. We need some more time just to sit and visit, ja?"

"Ja," Cheryl said with a smile. The two were laughing their way across the street when the unthinkable happened, an explosion so loud it rattled the windows and even broke a few as car alarms went off and people screamed.

Instinctively Cheryl dropped to her knees and pulled Naomi with her. Though prayers were going through her head, it wasn't the reason why she got on her knees. She just felt like they needed to be lower to the ground, which continued to tremble and shake.

"What was that?" Naomi asked, her eyes wide.

Not quite confident that it wouldn't happen again, Cheryl eased back into a standing position. In the distance she could see smoke billowing as fire sirens wailed.

"I think... I think something exploded."

A NOTE FROM THE EDITORS

We hope you enjoyed Sugarcreek Amish Mysteries, published by the Books and Inspirational Media Division of Guideposts, a nonprofit organization that touches millions of lives every day through products and services that inspire, encourage, help you grow in your faith, and celebrate God's love.

Thank you for making a difference with your purchase of this book, which helps fund our many outreach programs to military personnel, prisons, hospitals, nursing homes, and educational institutions.

We also create many useful and uplifting online resources. Visit Guideposts.org to read true stories of hope and inspiration, access OurPrayer network, sign up for free newsletters, download free e-books, join our Facebook community, and follow our stimulating blogs.

To learn about other Guideposts publications, including the best-selling devotional *Daily Guideposts*, go to Guideposts.org/Shop, call (800) 932-2145, or write to Guideposts, PO Box 5815, Harlan, Iowa 51593.

Sign up for the
Guideposts Fiction Newsletter
and stay up-to-date on the books you love!

You'll get sneak peeks of new releases, recommendations from other Guideposts readers, and special offers just for you . . .

and it's FREE!

Just go to Guideposts.org/Newsletters today to sign up.

Guideposts.®